Penguin Books
Girls at Play

Paul Theroux was born in Medford, Massachusetts, in 1941, and published his first novel, *Waldo*, in 1967. He wrote his next three novels, *Fong and the Indians*, *Girls at Play* and *Jungle Lovers*, after a five-year stay in Africa. He subsequently taught at the University of Singapore and during his three years there produced a collection of short stories, *Sinning with Annie*, and his highly praised novel *Saint Jack*. His other publications include *The Black House* (1974); *The Great Railway Bazaar: By Train Through Asia* (1975), an account of his adventurous journey by train from London to Tokyo and back; *The Family Arsenal* (1976); *The Consul's File* (1977); *Picture Palace* (1978, winner of the Whitbread Literary Award); *A Christmas Card* (1978); *The Old Patagonian Express: By Train Through the Americas* (1979); *World's End and Other Stories* (1980); *London Snow* (1980): *The Mosquito Coast*, which was the *Yorkshire Post* Novel of the Year for 1981 and the joint winner of the James Tait Black Memorial Prize; *The London Embassy* (1982); *The Kingdom by the Sea* (1983); *Doctor Slaughter* (1985); *Sunrise with Seamonsters: Travels and Discoveries 1964–1984* (1985), *O-Zone* (1986) and *Riding the Iron Rooster* (1988).

Paul Theroux divides his time between Cape Cod and London.

Paul Theroux

Girls at Play

Penguin Books

PENGUIN BOOKS

Published by the Penguin Group
27 Wrights Lane, London w8 5tz, England
Viking Penguin Inc., 40 West 23rd Street, New York, New York 10010, USA
Penguin Books Australia Ltd, Ringwood, Victoria, Australia
Penguin Books Canada Ltd, 2801 John Street, Markham, Ontario, Canada l3r 1b4
Penguin Books (NZ) Ltd, 182–190 Wairau Road, Auckland 10, New Zealand

Penguin Books Ltd, Registered Offices: Harmondsworth, Middlesex, England

First published in Great Britain by the Bodley Head Ltd 1969
First published in this edition by Hamish Hamilton Ltd 1978
Published in Penguin Books 1983
10 9 8 7 6 5

Made and printed in Great Britain by
Richard Clay Ltd, Bungay, Suffolk
Filmset in Monophoto Plantin

**For my parents,
with love**

'At my request we took a two hours' walk in the forest, following a very narrow and almost invisible path, while a native armed with a stick preceded us to clear the way. Interesting as this walk was, amongst the unfamiliar vegetation, I must confess I am a little disappointed with the forest. I hope to find better elsewhere. The trees are not very high; I expected more shade, more mystery and strangeness . . .'

ANDRÉ GIDE, *Travels in the Congo*

Contents

I
The Playing Field

The flame trees enclosed the hockey field in a high leafy wall of bulging green; rotting orangey-red blossoms littered the moist grass. The setting sun, spattered over half the sky, made patches in the ordered field precisely gold. Beyond a straight row of blue gums, but out of sight, a bog with a stream cutting through it housed a motley orchestra of swamp-dwellers tuning up for the night. On all sides of the field were green juicy barriers; an African cage, comfortable and temporary.

If the fat black girls had not been there and playing, the order of this playing field in the highlands of East Africa would terrify. The order seemed both remote and unreasonable. Explorers have come upon abandoned buildings deep in Africa and suddenly felt despair, confronted by roofless walls, broken lizard-cluttered stairs, solid doorways opening on to dense ferns and dark towering trees. A discernible order in a place where there are no people (the dry mosque in the dunes) is a cause for alarm; it means failure; the decaying deserted order is a gravemarker.

The delighted squeals of the girls at their game, the whacking of sticks, the ball being cracked across the grass, gave the order a reason for existing. The playing field stayed a cage, and the sun moving down, drawing all its yolk with it, darkened it; but the girls were enjoying their two hours. For the black, large-buttocked girls at the school, there was nothing to worry about. In their green bloomers and grey jerseys, which showed their swinging unsupported breasts, they ran heavily-hunched and held their sticks low, yelping cheerfully.

The game had just started; now the girls' voices were loud, the motion of their squat bodies was unusually vigorous in no specific direction. They were playing on a regulation-size hockey field, they had good equipment and wore uniforms, but the game was clearly chaotic and lacking in suspense. The game was an end; no one tried to score. It was not a question of the game going well – the game always went well. The motion was important, it allowed the girls a chaste outlet for their mindless energy. It was the reason for the orderly playing field hacked out of the bush. It gave the girls two hours of caged supervised play. This was Miss Poole's idea; it also gave the teachers a chance to have tea or a sundowner, to visit each other, have a siesta and generally forget that they were in the East African bush, over two hundred corrugated miles from Nairobi and not married.

Miss Verjee, the Games Mistress, worked these two hours. She watched the girls at play. An Indian (her father manufactured nails in Kampala), athletic except for her bowed Asian legs, she had a year before earned her teaching certificate from a rural teacher training college. She hated the girls, feared Miss Poole and was uncertain about her teaching. She knew she would not be at the school much longer; as she stood there on the playing field watching the hockey game, her parents were arranging a marriage for her.

Out of the corner of her eye Miss Verjee saw a small white figure nestled in the bushes on the far fringe of the playing field. The white figure did not move. It sat, ghostly in a still hedge, squinting at Miss Verjee.

Miss Verjee grasped at her whistle.

Like tired dancers the girls started to drop sighing to the field. Six lay on their backs in the grass. Miss Verjee commanded them to get up. One looked at her and then fell back heavily, flinging her hockey stick to the side. Miss Verjee blew her whistle and walked angrily towards those who had stopped playing and fallen down. As she approached the six she saw others at the far goal sit on their haunches and grin at her. She blew her whistle again and shouted for them to rise. Now all the girls flopped down and as they did Miss Verjee looked back once at the silent white figure, the dwarf at the far end of the field who, Miss Verjee knew, was taking it all in. In a strident voice which retained the Kutchi rhythms, rising and falling like a frantic prayer, Miss Verjee called, 'Get *up*, you *girls*! It is *not* the half-*time*!'

The girls did not move. On the field, patched gold and green, they could have been dark chess figures, checked into immobility by the ugly white queen squatting at the far end. The wind shushed in the flame trees, and then there was a voice.

'Thees woman ees useless.'

'Who *said* that?'

Miss Verjee took a girl by the arm and demanded to know if she had said it. The girl laughed, others laughed, and then from a group of hunched-over girls came a high excited yodelling, as from a tribal dance. Miss Verjee panicked. Holding the girl and drawing her up, Miss Verjee hit her hard across the face. The girl pulled away roughly, scrambled to her feet, and began running in the direction of Miss Poole's house.

'The rest of you *play*!' shrieked Miss Verjee, chasing the girl. None of the girls moved or spoke; they watched the bow-legged Indian chasing the short fat African across the green field, the steps making a moist squash-squash-

squash in the grass. Miss Verjee caught the girl easily at the sideline and held her. 'Where do you think you are going?'

'You heet me,' said the girl, looking to the side sullenly. 'I weel tell Miss Poole.'

'Not now,' said Miss Verjee. She could not control her nervousness and was out of breath. 'You are supposed to be playing, don't you see?'

The girl said nothing. She folded her arms. Both teams, flat on the ground, stared at Miss Verjee who, facing the girl, blocked the path to Miss Poole's.

'What do you *want*? You disobeyed me. What shall I *do*? You know you can't see Miss Poole now. It's playtime.'

'I am going.'

'Miss Poole is expecting the new teacher. You can't see her.'

'Yes.' The girl tried to pull away but Miss Verjee held her fast.

'*Please.*' Miss Verjee had promised herself that she would not use that word. It came out quickly and she regretted it as soon as she heard it. 'Don't.'

The girl's smooth black face was expressionless. Even the eyes, brown-blotched and narrowed, revealed nothing. She turned without a word and walked back to where her friends lay like casualties.

Miss Verjee knew she had done more than she should. But it was worth it. Miss Poole would not be disturbed. She put her steel whistle in her mouth and blew a shrill *tweee*. Then in her high helpless voice called:

'*Half-time!*'

2
Miss Poole

Miss Poole was sitting in her room awaiting the vulgar knock of the intruder. She was alone with her prickly reverie: the same room for fifteen years. She quickly corrected the thought – not that particular room, but in that kind of room; and for the past seven years the room had been in East Africa. The previous eight, a sad pause, had been spent in a room in London and, before that, twenty-five happy years in the sun, in the highlands of East Africa. It had been a short life; now she thought of it as mostly over, only a few more years left: the surprise of ease and happiness at the beginning, now the close gloom of walls and the uncomfortable knowledge that she was about to be intruded upon.

She did not think of the years in numbers, seven years back in East Africa after an eight-year absence in England. Not in numbers – rather, in blocks of time made out of light and joy or darkness and strain, all of which created in her sensations she could phrase very simply. If someone asked her how long she had spent in England she replied, 'Too long' and that was that. Sometimes she added, 'A shocking place. Absolutely shocking.' The length of time she had spent in East Africa she explained by saying, 'I was born here.' The simple statement was given a greater importance by her looks: she was forty but could easily have been taken for sixty. Her clear eyes were in queer contrast to her dry skin, her frumpy brown frocks and her hairstyle that appeared deliberately plain. She had no wish to look young, and her apparent creaking age was an advantage, for she knew that the old were not required to compete.

Nowadays people very seldom asked Miss Poole questions. It seemed as if the Americans were the only ones who had ever bothered to wonder, and there were few Americans around. They had asked in their curious way, 'You mean to say you were *born* here?'

Miss Poole preferred not to think about it.

But she could not ignore her room. What worried her was that from where she was sitting she could see that the room was slowly cracking, showing shrivelled rents, coming apart and falling away from her. Soon, she imagined, it would fall completely and leave her unprotected. Those on the outside, and not all Africans, had weakened it with their insistent knocks. The Africans ignored the fact, or did not care, that all doors had been open to them for the past seven years. Their revenge was not complete in the knowledge that they could enter anywhere and take over. They wanted to tear the whole place down.

They rattled the windows (Miss Poole heard them at night); they tapped on the walls in a threatening code (often Miss Poole had shone a flashlight out of the window and watched their shadowy figures disappearing with arrogant slowness into the trees, their knives flashing); they tried the doors, trampled the flowers, snatched underthings from the clothes-line and upset the trashcan grubbing for papers. They kicked at the cats and made gabbling noises at Julius in the kitchen. Once she had heard them creak across her tin roof, bumping their knees and toes on the rippled tin and making a fearful metallic juddering. The racket that accompanied this roof incident was horrible for

Miss Poole lying face up and helpless on her bed, knowing that they were above her, probably naked, a few feet away, armed with machetes and trying to get in. She replaced the tin roof with tiles.

Miss Poole's one consolation was that the poor dears never seemed to be able to do anything right, not even burgle a house. But this was a small comfort, for when she heard them she did not stir, she lay in her bed malarial with fright. They usually went away. It was suicide to face them. She had seen a thief lunge at her father who was holding a shotgun and fired into the thief's screaming mouth, opening his face up – a wet stringy hole – with the blast.

When intruders came she prayed, and fatigue's blessed mechanism would work on her and send her into unconsciousness before dawn. Long ago, in her youth, the sun had calmed her, but these past seven years had been awful. There were days when she refused to leave her room to go into other parts of the house, days when she did not go to the office or teach her classes, days when she could not bring herself to look out of the window, worn out from keeping awake the whole night, stiff, hot, anxious and awaiting the violent ripping of her knotted unvoiding bowels by the sharp tool of an intruder.

The night before had been like that and now she sat in her room, trying to rest in safe dusty daylight, squeezing her irritation between her palms. Her whole head was rigidly staring, her gaze was fixed on her office in the stone building across the hedged lawn of the compound. She knew why she had been scared and could not sleep: there had been a nightmare intruder, not an African, but a white woman.

That had been a nightmare; it had kept her from sleeping. Today the intruder would arrive. The previous day a letter had come from the Ministry of Education. Miss Poole had expected the usual ungrammatical circular ('It has came to my atention ...') and so slit open the envelope with indifference. The envelope still read ON HER MAJESTY'S SERVICE, although East Africa had been independent for seven years. It was not a smudged circular; it was a letter from the Chief Education Officer.

Dear Madam,
Notice of transfer: Heather Monkhouse
Ref. your letter D/22/67 of 11th inst. requesting English teacher.

This is to inform you that as from 24 Jan., 1967, Miss H. Monkhouse, formerly of Lord Mainwaring Girls' School, Nairobi, is transferred to your employ. She is expected to take up her duties immediately and has been notified to arrive on the above date. Her subjects are English and drama.

Her Confidential File etc. has been sent via registered post.

Miss Poole was elated. She had not expected a prompt reply to her request; teachers were so hard to get up-country. No one wanted to come to the bush.

'Simon!'

'Madam.'

'Did a registered packet arrive this morning?'

'Yes, madam.'

'You might have had the good sense to bring it to me.'

'Madam?'

'*Leta* important *baruha pesi-pesi*,' demanded Miss Poole. The elation had worn off; such feelings did not survive the heat. Miss Poole prayed for simple patience; it was the middle of the morning – by noon the temperature would be in the nineties. Above her head bits of sawdust snowed down from the wooden roof beams: white ants. The sawdust gathered on her blotter with ugly subtleness, like dandruff on a collar.

Simon placed a foolscap-size folder, fuzzed with rolls of lint from constant rubbing, over the whorls of dust. He left the office in silence.

Momentarily, Miss Poole's elation returned. The folder was unusually thick, filled with dog-eared letters, onion-skin carbons of directives, reports and ministry documents strung together on a frayed piece of green cord. She flipped through the bundle quickly, then placed the folder flat, opened to the top letter and read. She read only four pages before she slammed it shut (it huffed dust), kicked her chair back and called for Simon.

'Take this away,' she ordered stiffly. 'And unless you do something about those ants I shall be looking for a new clerk. Is that clear?'

'Madam?'

Miss Poole began impatiently repeating the same words in Swahili, but half-way through broke into English saying, 'Can't *any*one do *any*thing right!' and clopped out of her office to her house, her room, where she knew she would be safe. Her room was close with peace and fragrance, but this would not last; the woman was on her way.

3
Heather

Her lingering memory was of an elderly methodical gent in Croydon who had made love to her in the way a man might eat a soft-boiled egg. Heather had watched him do both. If there was a difference it was in frequency: he had an egg every day, but demanded her less often. Each time he took her (only fleshless verbs occurred to her: *had*, *took*, seldom *made love*) she watched him carefully, in silence. He picked at her with the tips of his fingers. He flaked off bits and rubbed them with his thumb. He peeled, prodded her smooth shell and all the while stared at what he was doing. For over three months Heather stared with him. Her metaphor never changed. She even worked out elaborate sexual imagery: the Male, spoon in hand, hunched over a warm egg; the shell picked slowly off with blunt fingers and broken nails, the membranous skin peeled and smoothed. He worked slowly and Heather was always amazed to discover that during this preliminary her desire heightened, she became hungry. And so did he: he cooed breathy nonsense, his eyes popped, his mouth fell open, his tongue protruded. Then the dunking of the spoon, the gooey yolky mass trembling.

The image of the soft-boiled egg, instead of diminishing the vividness of the act, made it seem more passionate and easier to recreate. It gave an acceptable form to something she looked upon in England with uncertainty. She liked doing it, but it seemed healthier not to think about it always in the same naked way. Most of all, her image was private, a guarded secret: it was all the privacy she had. She clung to this single perception as if to a fragile antique: she, the ravished egg, scraped clean, spooned of her juices, emptied in a cute little cup, with scraps of yolk, a soiled spoon and the remnants of broken shell littering a plate some distance from a still, satisfied man.

The jerky motion of her V W jouncing at sixty over the corrugated back roads always made her think of sex; it hurt her, and even the safe image gave her little relief. For days she had thought of nothing but her recent humiliation. The V W's sexy rhythms did not help matters, for driving she thought of love and how either party was able to turn the trust of love into violation and, in time, ridicule. At any moment, with something as simple as a careless gesture, a man could make a whore of his lover.

Heather winced. Well, she thought, wasn't it pleasant with that nice old man in Croydon? Such a dear he had been: quiet, considerate, discreet (before he pushed off he put his slippers, his toothbrush, his hot-water bottle and pyjamas in his briefcase and kissed her on the forehead: no harm done). He was nothing like the bastard in Nairobi – Heather refused to think of his name, but it came against her will – Colin. She had, after knowing him some while, made a joke about the name, the point of which was 'because you're so anal', but he had not found it very funny and replied angrily with something irrelevant and rude. Heather had never seen this in him before but it provided an explanation to something that had been bothering her. This rude impulse of Colin, just one random insult, seemed to explain his early marriage and now his excessive un-happiness at being married. When he was out with Heather and making love it was performed with the married man's directness, artlessly and in silence. He had never said much about his wife, but for that brief moment Heather had assumed the wife's taunting role, was insulted, and it became clear to her why the whole affair, like so many others (but excluding the kindly old egg-eater in Croydon), was hopeless. If she became the wife for a few mocking moments, Colin became the husband, and she knew as soon as he made the reply that she should break it off. She had said, 'Are you trying to tell me something?' He was silent. But it was a warning, and she knew humiliation would follow.

It had before. Heather thought of herself as a girl, and dressed like one, but she was a woman of thirty-six who had had on the average one and a half affairs every year since she was twenty-five. She had a capacity for disaster that was written bluntly in a cuneiform of small scars all over her body. Most of her affairs began just before Christmas when everyone seemed friendly, were consumated on New Year's Eve ('Let's start the New Year off right,' many of the men had said), and went completely to pieces in the spring. Those were the English ones, largely influenced by the foul weather and the difficulty of meeting people casually, or at all, except at large parties. Heather's job as a salesgirl in the 'Stork Shoppe' in the Croydon branch of an Oxford Street store made it impossible for her to meet men; she sold only maternity wear and when men did come into her department their most remote thought was of picking her up. Heather always considered it the worst place to be: none of the men even looked at her and she was aware that, because of her particular job, the men assumed that she was in the early stages of pregnancy herself. And instead of kindling an interest in motherhood, the job convinced Heather that children were the last thing she wanted. The distended women that shopped were flushed or blotched, vacant-eyed, flatulently lumbering among the clothes-racks, rubbing the flowered tent-like frocks between their cold fingers; their husbands looked away, distractedly praying. The few men that shopped alone ignored her; she had to wait for the Christmas parties, and she dreaded the coming of spring.

It was against all poetry, but poetry was rubbish. Love was two friends disembarrassing themselves in a bed, not handholding in Kew Gardens. In spite of all odes, love and the lies that went with it appeared in the winter, indoors, after dark. By spring the friendship was finished and, as with Colin, a signal was given, a futile rudeness which meant that it would all be over soon. The men had been rude, never Heather. And each time, Heather had asked a testing question to find out if the insult was intended. The men seldom replied, but Heather knew they had been trying to tell her something. She could not stand the thought that she would be left again; she always let the warning pass. But after two or three times she grew to recognize these hard scarring words which were uttered long before the actual parting; they made the last months terrible and the parting itself a predictable misery.

She had come to Africa five years before to get away from it all: the filthy crowded subways, the sooty church steeples, the wilted working-class faces she saw everywhere, the swollen women who shopped in her department. When the man in Croydon put his toothbrush and pyjamas into his briefcase, kissed her coolly on the forehead and said, 'Cheerio, my dear, keep your pecker up', Heather looked into a mirror, detected signs of wear and decided to go to Spain. She needed a *fiesta*.

But with the English equivalent of only a few hundred *pesos* the *fiesta* would not be a long one, she knew. A friend suggested a Mediterranean cruise because 'one never knows what might happen to one on a cruise'. The friend hinted at the unknowns and Heather calculated coldly all the possibilities in a little mental log: there would be sex, after a few days at sea everyone would be screaming for it, possibly on a moonsplashed deck, more likely assignations below deck ('We could go to my compartment – It's quieter there and I could slip into something more comfortable . . .'); there would be cocktail parties at the Captain's table, costume balls, games of shuffleboard and deck tennis, lots of vino and perhaps another go at *Anna Karenina*. Everyone knew what cruises were like. But Heather did not want a cruise, she wanted a life. Like Spain, the cruise would end and, even if it did not end disappointingly, depression would follow. After the holiday she would have no money; there would be a let-down, comfortless brooding, her heart and purse emptied out. Still she knew she had to leave England, and soon; the Christmas meeting, the inevitable New Year's episode and the spring collapse had been so regular – and now an almost glandless ritual – that Heather recoiled from the thought of December.

She did not send Christmas cards that year. She avoided the Christmas ads in the paper and, when holly appeared on the teller's cage, stopped going to the bank. Without being fully conscious of it she scanned the classifieds, and one day read a large framed ad about teachers being wanted in East Africa. The ad was half a plea and half a travel brochure. 'Teachers', it said, 'are sorely needed by the children of deprived farmers in the cool upland plateaux near the breathtaking slopes of the majestic volcanic mountains of East Africa. Struggling for an education the African child often must walk 15 or 20 miles through incredibly green meadows and thick pine forests in his bare feet. The fauna and flora are of a kind rarely

seen outside the spectacular and seldom-visited ...'
Heather read on to the last sentence which ended, '... you
would be rendering valuable service to East Africa, now
on the threshold of independence.' Heather reflected on
the ad. She was not a teacher, but the store had once sent
her on a day-release course to study mothercraft and a little
bit of domestic science; she had done well in the course
and the manager even spoke of sending her to Bath for a
diploma. She could supply reasonably good references;
the old egg-eater would write an enthusiastic one. And she
spoke English, an added advantage, since this would give
her another subject to teach the poor people in the green
upland plateaux. Heather wondered if it was East Africa
where that exotic love story took place, the romance on the
equatorial plantation between the wealthy tea planter with
the Daimler and the girl that had just come out from
England on a visit. 'I knew you were British,' the silver-
haired planter had said to the girl; 'you have ice in your
heart that wants thawing.' They had made love in a room
smelling of blossoms. Outside, the roar of the monsoon.

After a strenuous physical (no one asked her about the
mothercraft lessons) and many warnings (the friend who
had recommended the cruise said, 'Don't come back with
a black man'), Heather signed a four-year contract and
boarded the *Prince of Wales* bound for Mombasa. It was in
many ways the cruise she had reflected on earlier; there
were costume balls, dance competitions and several pro-
posals to go 'just below to my cabin' from unattached men.
Heather turned down all but one. The man was insistent,
very strong and rather slow-witted, and the most per-
suasive words he spoke were not about the delights of
going below but that in a week's time the ship would be
calling at Aden and he would be getting off: his wife and
children were waiting for him there. It was the speedy,

private, uncluttered affair Heather badly wanted. Calculating their movements with a precision she lyingly attributed to the man, she managed the whole business with elaborate secrecy and made the man believe in his heart that he had plotted it all. He gave Heather his elephant-hair bracelet as a souvenir and left at Aden as he said he would. Heather was happy. A little caution had made the trip pleasant and now she could arrive in East Africa alone and completely free, like the English girl in the exotic story.

As the *Prince of Wales* left Aden and drew closer to the East African coast, the passengers began drinking heavily, staying up later; and they became friendlier, closer, offering stories to testify to their good intentions. With her man gone, Heather had more free time and spent part of the day and much of the evening in the ship's bar. The men took an interest in her that was protective rather than romantic. They made an effort to let Heather listen to the stories because, as they told her, she had never been to Africa before and had not the slightest idea of what it was like to live in a country populated with savages. The stories were of unrelieved horror made even more horrible for Heather when she said, 'Oh, but I'm rather like that English girl in the Maugham story. Very lucky, you know. I'll meet a tea planter and he'll see me through!'

'I read that story,' a man put in. 'It wasn't about East Africa.'

'You must be mistaken,' said Heather. 'It was the tropics, and Nairobi was mentioned, I'm sure.'

'You're way off,' another man said. 'That was Singapore or somewhere in Malaya. There were *punkawallahs* mentioned in that book. We don't have *punkawallahs* in East Africa.'

'You don't?' Heather spoke in a tiny voice.

'Nope, not a one.' The man grinned.

'You see,' said a man sitting close to Heather, 'the Malayans have a reasonably interesting culture. They brought bananas to Africa – they had boats, they travelled. But I'll tell you something. Civilization started in East Africa, right in Olduvai Gorge, not far from my place.' The man swigged his beer and smacking his lips added, 'It started there, and that's where it stopped.'

'In the arsehole of the Empire,' said a man across the room into his frothy tankard.

Heather was crushed. They talked of East African brutality, a bloody outpouring of atrocity stories which trapped Heather in worry and made it impossible for her to stir. She began to hate herself for having signed the contract. She felt like a fool; she knew she could have stayed in London, continued working, and gone on as before. She thought with remorse of the missed opportunity for breaking the depressing pattern of loveless affairs. She might easily, she considered, have rid herself of it all. And even if she had gone back to the same thing, what the men in the ship's bar were describing was something much worse than any fear she had known: those June days in England were empty, but it was a familiar emptiness and, as bad as it had ever been, there were still memories of kindness. Another Christmas might have caused her unhappiness, she knew that; but she might have found a man as well.

Africa repelled her now. The *Prince of Wales* was three days out of Aden; Heather started throwing up. She did not let on that she was sick; she kept her aplomb by smiling at the drunks in the bar and saying, 'If you'll excuse me, I really must move off to the ladies' loo to spend a penny' and then she would go to her cabin and retch violently. Sometimes she would be overcome by the heaving and spend the night gasping on her bunk, utterly

25

exhausted, spewing green bile into her tin pail. Africa, the life she had thrown away, the decision she had made in a moment of foolish haste, the horrible stories – it all sickened her. Heather began to imagine Africa a huge black carcass, inert in the ocean, with evil at its centre, and all Africa's vastness radiating mishap off its shores in dark smelly eddies.

The sickening vision became fact. After one terrible night in her narrow compartment sensing the awful splashing, Heather went to the map outside the dining-room and saw that the red-knobbed pin which represented the ship had not moved. Every morning she had examined the map; every day the pin had moved closer to Mombasa on a route of pin-hole punctures that had very nearly cut the map in half. But the pin had not moved; it was stuck in the Gulf of Aden where it had been the previous day. Her vision had been true. The ship was being repelled by Africa's plastic evil as Heather had been repelled by the stories of Africa's pointless brutality; the ship had stopped and was being thrust away. Heather lay on her bunk and puked into the pail.

The trip to Aden had been done in almost record time, but now less than 1,500 miles out of Mombasa the *Prince of Wales* developed trouble with the port screw. A type-written notice tacked next to the map said there would be 'a slight but unavoidable delay due to engine difficulties ...' No one seemed to mind. Instead of the horror stories there was now great mirth in the bar, as there had been at Gibraltar and Port Said, shouted exchanges about never getting to Mombasa, about being towed back to Aden and staying drunk. There were jokes about what could be wrong, which included the word screw in the punchline.

Heather listened to them all and smiled with the men. She did not want anyone to know of the fears that made her continually sick. Once she even added a screwing joke of her own (a limerick about the man from Timbuktoo) and was yipeed. But after two days of joking about the varieties of screws, the horror stories began again, each one prefaced by, 'We're giving you the real Africa – not that shit you read about in poovey books.' With the ship listing uncomfortably Heather sat on a bar-stool licking her pink gin, not commenting, though encouraging the men by inquiring after details about Africans and frowning in genuine concern.

For a reason Heather at first could not even guess at, the returning settlers and expatriate civil servants suspected her of being sympathetic towards Africans. Heather was sorry they felt that way, embarrassed knowing this and also knowing the details of the stories about Africans they were telling her. She wanted to give the impression that she was not afraid and that she, like they, also disliked Africans; at the same time she knew with a deep private dread that she feared and hated Africa and Africans.

The suspicions of the people in the ship's bar were founded on an incident Heather had forgotten; it had been a very slight thing, but everyone knew about it. She had spoken to a soft-voiced African at Palermo who monotonously explained that he had bought a little crucifix and been cheated by the Italian at the sidewalk stand. Heather put him wise to the Italians, whom she called 'Eye-ties', but as she said this word she realized that she would give a hundred blacks for one Italian – in fact, she had been loved by an Italian just a year before. The absurdity of describing a nationality she distrusted to a man she knew she loathed struck her at once. She giggled and told the African to watch out because 'the wogs start at Calais'. The African thanked her for her advice and went away with the crucifix in his hand. The conversation had not lasted a minute. The next day everyone seemed to know about it and several people in the bar asked Heather if she thought Africans were people in the same way the English were people. Heather answered quickly and truthfully, no, she didn't think they were. Nothing specific was said until, during the time the port screw was being replaced, she got on more than joshing terms with the men in the ship's bar; one evening a man said to her drily, 'The ones that carry books scare me more than the real savages. Like that black you were chatting up when we went ashore at Palermo . . .'

She knew she was not prepared for Africa; she knew she was a tense, frightened unmarried woman with less than half her looks left. The trip had not done anything for her: her hair was snarled from the salty wind; her elbows were hard and scaly; her eyebrows had grown out and a cold sore had started on her lower lip. She hated this ugliness and hated herself even more for her foolish weakness in going away from where she had been at least safe. Alone, so far away, among strangers there could be no comfort. Her throat ached from retching and over-drinking; her nostrils were filthy from chain-smoking. And just before the *Prince of Wales* docked in Mombasa she had a fleeting thought of the terrible mistake she had made in letting the strong dull man go back to his wife in Aden. She might have made promises, told lies, blackmailed him; she might have convinced him to come with her and make her safe. She walked down the clattering gangway trembling, into the humid reeking town, a sob stuck in her throat: she wanted that man back.

'Lots of rain,' the Major said. It was the first full sentence he had spoken all evening. He said it directly to Heather.

'It doesn't look that way,' said Heather. She smiled and

sipped her gin. She knew no one at the table; she had come to the club with the Major, a tanned athletic man of about fifty whose only bad point, as far as Heather could tell, was the hair growing out of his ears. He had said he was a policeman and Heather had laughed, 'A *white* policeman in a *black* country.' The Major said there were stranger things in East Africa than that and chatted with her at her hotel before asking her politely if she would like to meet some of his friends. East Africa, he said, was a small place; she would get to know nearly everyone eventually. That was how things were. She had been in Mombasa only a day and had had a restful night (a sweeper had bowed and said, 'I will clean now, my ladyship' in the morning; this she found reassuring). Now she found herself among strangers, but she was not unhappy. She felt almost relaxed and not very worried; it was night and, with the tropical foliage in darkness, like Cornwall in summer. The exactitude of this association gave the outpost a familiarity and calmed her even more. She drained her glass and saw the Major moving closer to her.

'No,' he said, 'a good eight inches more than last year.' He spoke quietly, as if he did not want the others to hear.

Heather was mildly confused. She did not know what he was talking about. The path to the club veranda was bone-dry; and even from where she sat she could hear the scrape and rattle of palm fronds rubbing. The grass near the hotel had been sparse and brown, the open drains full of dead leaves and dry scraps of paper.

'At the hotel I thought to myself: this must be the dry season they're always talking about,' said Heather.

'In Mombasa,' said the Major.

'Yes. But you say you're getting lots of rain?'

The Major's face emptied. He stared at Heather and said, 'Didn't you say you're English?'

'Heavens, *yes*!' Heather looked around. No one was paying any attention to her.

'Well, I heard on the wireless this morning that there's masses of rain in the South. Sussex alone got six inches.'

'I was on the,' Heather tossed her head, 'the ship, you know.'

'They're talking of doing something about better drainage if it keeps on like this,' said the Major with concern. '*Lots* of rain. Worst in years.'

Heather asked the Major when he had last gone on home leave.

'Eleven years ago. Went home to bury my mother, stayed three weeks. England – you can have it, love. A bloody *shenzi* place.' The Major drank for the rest of the evening without speaking.

Around midnight a radio was produced. After a great deal of knob-twirling and antenna-adjusting, a sputtering crackling cricket match issued from the torn cloth of the loudspeaker. The Major seemed interested in the match, but Heather suggested leaving.

They went to his house. It was near the ocean and Heather could hear the waves crashing on the reef from where she lay in the bed. The Major made love to her slowly, silently, as if committing incest with his daughter. Afterward, Heather sat up in the dark; she held his head against her belly and whispered, 'Tomorrow I have to go to Nairobi. I have to be posted to a school and all that rubbish. Such a nuisance. I'd rather stay here with you. But I can't. I really can't.' She paused and closed her eyes. 'I don't want you to think I'm promiscuous or anything like that. You'll visit me, won't you? You have a car – it won't be too awful to drive up to . . .' The Major's head was heavy. Heather turned it slightly and saw that he was fast asleep.

★

Nairobi helped her forget it all. She felt as if she had never feared anything. The brutal stories continued, people talked of nothing else, but Heather no longer minded. She had become young, upper middle-class, desirable; men were good to her; her house in one of Nairobi's lovely suburbs was surrounded by flowers; there were servants. She felt confident, even wealthy; she never had to cook or clean. The nightmare of the ship, her fears and regrets, were forgotten in the ease of her present life. Her one sorrow was that she had not come sooner.

It was a fairy story, the gift of youth, with the same anxiety that fairy tales produce. Like the tale of the incredible longed-for wish, granted with a warning by the tall black genie, Heather's life in Nairobi came to have consequences which were more side effects than actual punishments. She had, a few weeks after arriving in East Africa, started using her outdated schoolgirl slang (she knew none other); often to her acute embarrassment she clowned; she began to drink heavily. But the gift was too great to let the few consequences matter.

The man in Croydon had once asked her what she wanted out of life.

'I want to be rich and famous, with men hounding me day and night. You know what I really want to be? A high-class call girl. Not a whore, you understand, but a paid girlfriend. I suppose that's every girl's dream. Which girl wouldn't trade places with Christine Keeler?'

In East Africa she got most of her wish. She was posted not to the cool upland plateaux but to a large girls' school in Nairobi. Nairobi was the most exciting city she had ever been in; she understood it, she felt she had a place there. Unlike London, it was filled with attractive people; no one was poor. There were bachelors everywhere, all doing exciting things (one of her lovers shot crocs, another had written the Five Year Plan). There were long gay parties which went on till dawn and finished with a dip in an embassy pool. The hairdressers, particularly one Italian lady who had come from Eritrea, were excellent – the best Heather had ever seen. She changed her hairstyle. She went out to eat nearly every evening and could open a menu and order with panache. Once in a while she sent food back to the kitchen and demanded to see the cook. She had wanted a new life; now she had one.

There was little to do at the school. She taught needle-work, home management and did Drama Club one after-noon a week. Sometimes she had an English class: the pupils read out loud from their books; Heather corrected their pronunciation. The school was run on the lines of a girls' school in England of thirty years ago, emphasizing discipline, good grooming, religious knowledge, and charm. All other things, with the exception of Latin and British History, came last; in seven years Heather never marked a student's paper. When she got depressed she had her hair done, dressed in her best clothes and, with one of her girlfriends, sat in the Thorn Tree sidewalk café nursing a gin and let herself be cajoled into accepting a drink from a tourist. She was delighted just watching the beautiful people strolling by in their light clothes: the tanned hunters, the young slim-legged girls with long soft hair. Africans were all around her, but she never saw them; she found she did not even have to hate them; they kept their distance.

Heather knew that she would never leave East Africa, although she was also certain that she would not allow herself to die there. For the foreseeable future, there was nowhere else to go; there were no more decisions to be made. She knew that her fears could come back, the retching could return; she shored herself up against unhappiness by refusing to get involved with a man and, like the call girl of her dreams, was businesslike in her affairs. There were many men but she seldom lost control and never fell in love. Love would have made life unbearable. Sex for her became a small moment set in days of fun; it was a quick unsatisfying fumble on a bed that provided no relief but was over in a matter of seconds and almost forgotten in a week. She expected nothing from it. She only made love to a man after she had got all she wanted from him and, with one disastrous exception, made this plain to the man beforehand. Her love affairs ended with the act of love, which was how she wanted it.

But there were times when an ended affair produced violence in her. More than mere bitchery, it was frankly vicious, and for no apparent reason she would find herself at home after the man left, screaming, crying, smashing things. If her servant intruded on her weeping she fired him. But the next day, or sometimes the next hour, she would become very calm and write letters to old girlfriends describing the unhappy affair in a succession of cheerful half-truths. This reduced her unhappiness by creating for her a different personality, gay and mature, and found only in the letters. These selected fictions stayed with her and it was these versions of her affairs she remembered. Often she tried to mime the perfect emotions she wrote. After the letters she would get into her car and drive around Nairobi, down the wide, palm-lined avenues, past the race course or out to the airport, until she was tired of driving. Outside the city, where the huge green continent began, she parked and turned from the twinkling city lights to the darkness of the night's empty distances. She had everything except love and she knew that pursuing love she would lose everything.

Heather had reached that point in unmarried life where

she tried not to think about what she was missing and would never have. She habitually consoled herself. Her dog, Rufus, was a bonus; she had not expected to like him: she had bought him on a whim three years before. She learned to take him seriously. His loyal affection, something she had taken for granted, now made her grateful. He had seemed a pointlessly gross hound, forever catching his tail in car doors and wounding his paws on stones. His size had conversational value, but except for that he had nothing: his eyes were rheumy, his tongue was raw and cracked, his teeth carious. Once or twice a year he had an attack of worms which made his ribs show and gave his jutting face an expression of listless panic, his eyes clouded, his jaw gaping. But none of this mattered to Heather. She had discovered in him a dumb sincerity she knew she lacked. This, with his stupid loyalty and his awkward maleness, she found touching. He was real; she knew she was not. She wondered whether Colin had been.

Only Rufus remained. There was no reason to think about Colin. She would never see him again. She was in her car, driving north with Rufus and everything she owned (many dresses, no furniture). Colin deserved nothing, not even a place in her memory, and she vowed out of bitterness not to think of the school she had just been forced to leave. The humiliation had been her own fault – bad timing, that was all. She had been telling herself lies. It didn't matter, nothing mattered, only the moving was important: now a new job, a distance, a different school. She could start again and not lose much. In East Africa it was not hard.

4
A Homecoming

The reverie of the room would not leave her: she was in a room and also imagining a tight box around her brain. The reality of one fed the despairing illusion of the other; it made her nightmare real. The cracked walls, the slumping shutters, the veils of cobwebs on the roof-beams, the plain decay of the room in which she was sitting caused that chamber of horrors in her imagination to become a hard image, a vision complete with discomfort and uncertainty, with dusty surfaces and loud noises, voices: a wall visibly cracking, the sound of a fist banging against the box, making it tremble. She could see herself, as if she were hovering above herself, staring down at the thin woman in the frayed chair, with her hands clasped prayerfully together and held against her sallow face, her elbows on her knees, her knees touching, feet some distance apart and pigeon-toed in brown thick-heeled shoes; the dress, an old dull cut, of fuzzy English woollen; her hair held in a bun with wisps trailing down which, at intervals, she flicked back with her fingers.

She had bathed, but smelled strongly of her cats. In spite of bathing every day and often twice a day, she always smelled of cats. But she did not find animal odours unpleasant. They were honest and did no harm. Miss Poole reasoned that only a person who was pretentious and vain would be conscious of his own smell and find shame in nature. She was not a woman of the world and had never tried to impress on anyone that she was anything but a farm girl, plain and practical, with a mind of her own and a tolerance for rough-necks and dung smells. The thought had crossed her mind years ago that if she ever had a husband (now the thought made her cringe) he too would have to tolerate, and perhaps even enjoy, the odours of animals, the ferret smells in damp undergrowth, the grainy odours of hens and heavy hairiness of farm dogs. Miss Poole did not notice an odour until it ripened into a stink. And she had always had pets: in her youth, hens; later, horses, dogs, rabbits, grey monkeys, and now, near the end of her life (this phrase rather than the figure forty), cats. Animal smells for Miss Poole existed quite apart from the concept of cleanliness. A mouldy orange was thrown out immediately; a mangy scabbed hound might scratch and moan for days, inches from where Miss Poole sat and stared.

There was a kind of order in the room, and a smell lingered about this too, because the order had been imposed by a succession of household pets. On her return from England after her eight-year absence she bought three dogs of undistinguished breed. The dogs had decided on the decor: where the chairs should be, how high the shelves should be, where the books should be kept (the dogs pawed and growled at the books; Miss Poole put the books in a back room). Tablecloths that didn't overhang, hairy throw-rugs, even plastic dishes instead of china were chosen because of the dogs' inclinations and not Miss Poole's. So it was an order that was not order, simply a queer consistency of the unbreakable, the shatterproof, the bite-resistant. Miss Poole was only following instructions.

She was happy this way. There were moments when her terror of the Africans left her, moments when, after her arrival back in East Africa, she sat and read a *Reader's*

Digest that was long out of date but clean, or times when she ate her bangers and mash – and these times she was happy that she had taken the risk and come back. While she read or ate or just sat in her chair the dogs sniffed at each other, pawed the carpet or sat beneath the dining table chewing hard at the fleas on the fur of their arse-flesh.

The cats a few years later made severe demands on her. The cats' insistence – particularly that of Sally, the oldest and largest – had been so firm that to obey their peculiar whim meant not only rearranging the sitting-room, but also getting rid of the dogs. Outside the house the cats played very well with the dogs. The girls at the school remarked on how well the beasts got along. Once inside the house there were snarls, glares; the cats hunched, bristling and hissing: the question of possession was raised. Miss Poole decided in favour of the cats, fixed up the room to suit them (clawing, kittens and soft sleeping places in corners had to be allowed for) and put the dogs in a house next to the servants' quarters where they terrorized the hens.

Miss Poole felt that her companionship with the animals was worthwhile because it was honest and predictable, and satisfying because it was not a substitute for human companionship (two canaries replacing one dead friend), but a satisfactory friendship that left humans out entirely. Miss Poole had no friends and seldom had visitors, except for the girls who came over occasionally for high tea. There was an absence of friends; but the animals with their smelly residues had not kept the friends away. She had always only had pets. As she grew older her pets had become progressively smaller (now she liked small cats). She could risk fairness with the pets and not be humiliated; she could stick to the rules and be rewarded for it.

Animals obeyed and could be trained and would respond as humans never did, for she saw in these creatures a helpless innocence bordering on holiness which did not exist in humans. There were times when she herself felt this bewildered helplessness which small animals showed. Unlike most humans there was no malice in the cats; while there were the usual subtle responses – many more than most people thought – there was no evil. They had not fallen. Man had. Much more than the high-voiced and man-crazy female, maggoty in the head and committing sins, these meek creatures were God's own.

Until she returned from her sad pause in England Miss Poole felt exactly the same about Africans. She had fed them and they responded in a manner that was both savage and innocent. Their undirected savagery was occasional, always inspired by people who wanted to change them. In her youth she had heard others speak of red-eyed wildness and murderousness, but Miss Poole had seen few instances of it. These she did not talk about, for she was no more interested in retailing the vulgarities of Africans than she would have been in describing the unfortunate household defecations of her pets.

When the eight years of confusion began in 1952 the Africans on her father's farm, faced with uncertainty and fearing for their lives, sought the reassurance of their employer and stayed inside the farm enclosure. They were more loyal than ever and the cane was rarely used, not because of political pressure (the Colonial Government was investigating alleged abuses) but because there was now no necessity for it. The Africans on the farm hated and feared the terrorists' insolence and, when trouble came to the farm, it was not Miss Poole's father (clutching his shotgun) or brother (a round-shouldered, mean-faced nail-biter) who did battle with the six intruders – naked men, yelping through the geraniums in the front garden and throwing stones at the side of the house – but two of the African workers. The workers were unmercifully slaughtered and left bleeding in the flowerbeds. Her brother went to South Africa shortly after; her father followed six years later.

Miss Poole's eight-year visit to England began the day after the attack on the farm. She was driven at great speed to the Nairobi airport; she flew to England where she met each member of the family, sometimes for tea, sometimes staying the weekend. At the end of two months she received no invitation to live at any of their houses. Rejected, though not displeased (she had no feeling for her relatives, but hated England with a hate that chilled and grimed her), Miss Poole spent the next eight years sitting in a number of rooms, usually alone, reading the *Geographical Magazine* and her Bible, knitting mufflers, doing the crossword, and putting shillings in the gas-meter.

In these cold rooms, odd mausoleums with the grey corpses stirring slightly, she dreamed of the order her father had given to a wild patch of African bush. The fenced stretches of green stayed in her memory, the animals and (quiet and numerous) the black men who had lived in the round brick huts near the kennel. In her tiny English room with vulgarities everywhere, a soiled rug, crumbs on the table, fingerprints around the light-switch (she could remedy none of these; she had always lived with servants and was incapable of even the smallest household task), she saw the huge plan of the farm for the first time in her life: the many barns and stables, the straight red roads and taut wire fences that sang like harps when the wind blew. She saw the order of the blocks of buildings, and the reason behind the order; the shop her father provided for the Africans where soap, salt, tea, sugar and small quantities of gin could be bought more cheaply than in town. A whole community, safe and green, which came alive when the morning bell sounded, the Africans scampering like hounds, chattering among themselves, making dark trails in thick dewy grass in their bare feet. Her father had brought all this to people who had lived bunched in disorder. The name Concord Farm had been given to the twenty thousand acres and it had prospered.

These were her dreams in England: not dreams of old friends, but of a situation, her home, which was for the moment beyond her reach. In this English tomb Miss Poole stopped living but aged twice as fast, a consequence she attributed to the cold and damp, and which her relations attributed to her bitterness and inaction. She knew that her relations would have mocked her horribly if they had known that in these dull rooms the inert and silent Miss Poole thought constantly of equatorial foliage, her soft pets, the gigantic pattern of the farm, and her happy days as a young girl in a land where the sun did not die. And what would the cousins have said if Miss Poole had explained her nostalgia: the warm caresses of a fat nursemaid who spoke reassurances to Miss Poole in Swahili? The vision of the woman's huge arms persisted: soft, black protective arms. And the woman had smooth cheeks and hard yellow palms.

Miss Poole flew back to Africa in 1960 and, when she arrived, wept. Worse than being a stranger, she was an enemy. She had decided that she wanted only to be anonymous in the sun with her small comforts; but she was not anonymous and she was hated. Before, people had said the Africans had no memories at all; now they said Africans had long cruel memories. As she passed through Customs and Immigration in Nairobi she saw that there was no longer a white man at the desk and not even a clear-eyed Sikh (efficient rustics and, for Miss Poole, the cleanest and most tolerable of the Asians in East Africa). There was an African in dark glasses who scraped his thick fingers over every page of her passport, was idiotically slow, set his mouth at her and instead of handing her the passport, rudely flipped it in her direction. It slapped on the floor; the African pointed an oversize finger at another traveller waiting to be processed. Miss Poole bent over for the passport. Her handbag dropped, spilling most of the contents: a brush and comb, a ballpoint, a wad of toilet paper, a compact, a small worn address book and diary, a half-eaten tube of fruit pastilles, some large loud English pennies. While she crouched and put this in order a magazine dropped and splashed on the stone floor (she could not remember how she had been carrying it). Confused by the humiliation, with her chest heaving against her knees making breathing difficult, she felt her throat constrict, started quickly away and heard an Americanized African voice shouting from behind. 'Hey, lady, you forgot dis.' She turned and saw her passport still on the floor. She went back and retrieved it (everyone in the lounge had heard the African; everyone watched her). Afterwards, she went straight to the ladies' room and burst into tears.

There were other incidents: an African in the hotel elevator (she could not tell if he was drunk, she could never tell with Africans) insisted on shaking her hand and telling her there was nothing 'to be fearing of black people – everyone is the same now, isn't it?' Later, a mis-understanding with a waiter she tried to tip: he thought she had raised her hand to strike him; he pulled away; a cup slipped from his tray and smashed; the saucer stayed. Avoiding the stares of an Asian family in the hotel corridor, she bumped her head on a supporting post and broke her sunglasses; the Asian man, despite her protestations that it was really nothing, uselessly tried to comfort her while the rest of his family watched Miss Poole in dark-eyed silence. Each time she wept in her room. There had never been Africans in the hotel and now there were many, in dark suits, talking together, each one eyeing her through a small white slit in a smooth black half-turned face. The thought struck her that an African might have slept in her very bed the night before. It was midnight when this occurred to her and she spent the rest of the night in a chair with a blanket wrapped around her, not sleeping, but thinking with sadness and anger of the violation the whole country had undergone. It was being trampled. From the first moment at the Customs and Immigration desk at the airport she had had the uneasy feeling that something was wrong, and now she knew: it was proved by her aching head and trembling hands. The whole place was undeniably fouled; but there was another plain truth which was worse than this: she was home.

Concord Farm had been sold. Some of the land was parcelled out to friends of the President who were already quarrelling over it. The farm buildings were part of an agricultural institute staffed by Americans from the Middle West. As crass and unresourceful as Africans, the Americans were pulling down the buildings, planting uneconomic crops and importing expensive farm machinery from America. This she gathered from the newspapers. She had known for some time that her father had joined her brother in South Africa; they were in Durban. Her father had sent a letter, but it was only after she arrived back in East Africa and had wept five or six times that the words of her father's letter came back to her.

She had received the letter while waiting for her sun-
less exile in the English room to end, and so anxious
had she been to preserve her soul-warming dream that
she had barely noticed it or did not dare understand it. In
the hotel room it returned to her, this time real and in
her father's own hoarse voice: '... Sold Concord to the
blacks ... good price ... only a fool wouldn't ... No
place here for a white ... Things are different now ...
About time I retired and wrote my memoirs, but there is
so much to tell I probably won't bother ... Isn't it
bloody? ...'

That was the second night in the hotel, the phrases
running through her head, mocking her fear ('... Only a
fool wouldn't ...') and extending her sleeplessness and
provoking tears in another unbearably bright day: her
memory of the sun was not this white fatiguing heat
which made a simple stroll a great effort. The crowds on
the sidewalk, the many tourists (Germans, of all people)
and all the Africans, who seemed to have money and
certainly were dressed well and undoubtedly in charge,
made the third day a nightmare. It was on the third day
that she resolved to leave Nairobi and go up-country,
anywhere green, where she could have flowers and pets,
pray and, if God was willing, continue living. She could see
the hills from the hotel window, the flatness which rose
slowly and dropped sharply to a valley forty miles across
where the earth had cracked and spewed up lava. There
would be few people in the highlands; only those who had
been born there could love it. The words of a hymn came
to her, all the roaring voices of farmers in a rustic church
singing in a children's service:

> Daisies are our silver,
> Buttercups our gold;

This is all the treasure
We can have or hold.

These shall be our emeralds –
Leaves so new and green;
Roses make the reddest
Rubies ever seen.

She could teach; a quiet mission station up-country
would be glad to have her, she thought. The next day she
hunted for a job. Though no mission schools existed – all
had been taken over by the Government – there were
many teaching jobs available. She sat in the Ministry of
Education and filled out forms. Each form demanded to
know what she had been doing for the past eight years,
where she had been, who would vouch for her. Many
unhappinesses were described on those forms; she shud-
dered just writing those several outer London addresses.
She was interviewed the same day and it went well,
even though the African conducting the interview left the
door to his office open and allowed many faces outside to
see Miss Poole nervously stammer answers. When the
African asked her what job she thought she was most
suited for, Miss Poole was surprised to hear herself say,
'I think a Headmistress – I would dearly love to head a
girls' school up-country. Education is such a terribly important thing in East Africa, and I would consider it an
honour...' She ran on. The African was no longer officious
but helpful, totally beguiled and even saying that in his
own district (Miss Poole recognized the name of the place:
she had been in a jumping competition there in the
Forties with her favourite horse, and had won a ribbon)
there was a girls' school which needed a Headmistress;
would Miss Poole consider that? His younger sister was
there, in Form Two. 'A very clever little chap,' he said.

44

Miss Poole smiled. Though she had not meant any affection by smiling and was only reacting to the word the African pronounced *clayver*, the African smiled back and shook her hand and grasped her thumb in the manner of a brother. Miss Poole said she would be most eager to take up her duties as soon as possible and added something to the effect that her lack of experience would be more than compensated for by her enthusiasm and, she said, 'zest'.

She had not thought of that for seven years, but for seven years there had been no serious intruders; there had been no need to reflect. In the bush, the school was out of danger, and changeless; the Ministry had always sent girls, and the girls had not stayed long. Today was different. Sitting in her chair, looking out of her window to the school compound, where the neatly pruned bougainvillea divided the hacked-out bush in a labyrinthine hedge of pure flowers, she recalled the words that were running through her head when she left the Ministry with the carbon of her signed contract. They sounded different now, very childish: *there will be flowers there*.

Miss Poole looked up and began to pray. She implored God with her heart. She stopped when she realized that she was looking not into Heaven but at a crack in the curved groin of the roof-beam. It was a new one; she had never seen it before. As her prayer subsided, the crack seemed to open and lengthen deliberately into a dark smirk.

5
The Memory of a Bitch

A long smooth patch of road, air rushing untroubled through the side-window, cleared Heather's head. The VW hummed along without bumping her mind back to men. Along the roadside, feeble decrepit shacks poked out from sturdy green foliage, huts squatted fouling delicious grass; here and there a flock of skinny mewling goats, a gap-toothed tribeswoman with a bundle of sticks on her head, a terrified hen flapping for its life. She was in the bush and she knew it by the awed stares of men standing in waist-deep grass, she knew it by the stupidity of the flea-bitten dogs sleeping in the middle of the road; a hundred miles into the forest, a thousand years back in time, now among people who uttered magic, dug with small pointed sticks, and with shards of glass circumcised little girls spread on mats.

Perfect for Miss Poole and bloody awful for everyone else, Heather thought, narrowing her eyes at the road ahead. Heather had heard a great deal about Miss Poole, but had met her only once, though memorably enough, at a conference for teachers in Nairobi.

'Isn't this the perfectly dreariest dullest thing you've ever seen!' Heather had said passionately to Miss Poole after one session.

Miss Poole had turned her grey face on Heather and said curtly, 'No. I don't agree. I think it's extremely useful. Our teachers need this sort of thing.'

'It bores *me* to tears.'

All the conference participants wore nameplates. Miss Poole looked at Heather's; Heather looked at Miss Poole's.

'You're a teacher?' asked Miss Poole, zipping her brief-case.

'Yes, I am.' Heather's voice was cold.

Miss Poole started to walk away, her mouth set colour-lessly in anger. She stopped, turned her head stiffly side-ways and, not quite looking at Heather, said without emphasis, 'It's a good job you're not at my school, young lady.'

Bitch, thought Heather. Now, with all her belongings in boxes tied to the roofrack, she was on her way to see Miss Poole, her new Headmistress. Heather laughed. Women did not frighten her; she knew what helpless madness they all felt. She knew what they wanted. The old ones were the worst of all. But working for Miss Poole would not have been easy in any case, even if she had never spoken to Miss Poole at the conference. And that had not been a blunder; she would have said some-thing like it eventually. She knew exactly where she stood, which was more than most people knew when they started a new job.

Everyone in Nairobi talked about Miss Poole. Some said she had slept with the Minister of Education in order to get her job. She could not have got it any other way, it was said. She was a failure, a ludicrously inefficient woman, a recluse at her own school. Many stories were told about her: having failed to collect fees one term, she had been accused of misappropriating funds and was forced to make up the difference from her own pocket; a hypochondriac, she spent days, weeks in her house moaning while a young Peace Corps girl acted as Head-mistress; and there was the story, told with some variations, of how the visiting Prime Minister discovered the national flag to be flying upside-down on the school flagpole. Miss Poole had made a public apology, but this was not enough; the Young Pioneers, the government youth brigade, forced her to carry a whole stalk of bananas on her head through the village market. So many stupidities.

But the school was small, remote and unimportant. Stupidities in the bush did not matter. People would tell stories, just as they told of outrages in the prisons; like the outrages, the stories of bush stupidities ('bush fever', some called it) could only be verified with great inconvenience. No one in East Africa would wish to take the enjoyment out of the stories by disproving them. If people gossiped about her Heather would never hear it. Nairobi was too far away.

Heather knew she had arrived at the school when, at the brow of a hill, she looked across the valley to a square collection of brown stone buildings, a queer order in all that jungle; the red-tiled roofs were redder, odder in the setting sun. The incongruity of a flag flapping in the mown quadrangle at the centre. To the side Heather saw a corner of the playing field, a green patch with black girls darting in and out of it with sticks. A stream ran along the far side of the compound, beyond a neat row of trees and a light green area that could only have been a papyrus swamp. For Heather it was a kind of detention camp – it even looked like one, with natural barriers of trees and water instead of barbed-wire fences. Heather was not hurt by the comparison; she preferred, at least for a while, the seclusion of a bush school to the further humiliation of living observed by gossips in Nairobi. She might be infuriated by the sewing-circle boredom; but she would hear no ridicule. Everyone down there under those red roofs was an embarrassment or they would not have been sent to the bush, like her. Heather could not disgrace the school; it was already in disgrace, and that had happened in Miss Poole's seven years.

As Heather descended the hill Rufus awoke, barking and slavering in the back seat. Heather told him sharply to lie down, but Rufus paid no attention. His head was out of the side window and the wind rushing by blew into his gaping mouth, curling his tongue sideways and making his loose jowls flap.

The VW jounced on the rutted puddly driveway and splashed towards Miss Poole's signboard.

6
Cat and Dog

Rufus sniffed at Sally and followed her around the lawn, bristling, making a prolonged growl in his throat. Miss Poole was at the window; Heather stayed in the car, teasing and fluffing her hair in the rear-view mirror, her eyes glassy with all the driving, lids dusted blue, her lips pressing several hairpins tight. From where she parked she could not see Rufus and the cat. She had not planned to let Rufus out of the car – he sometimes trotted away and stayed hidden for hours. He had tried but failed to get his large body through the window. He wagged his tail as he leaped around the back seat, lashing Heather's hair into a nest. 'Oh, damn,' Heather muttered and she opened the door. Rufus had made directly for Sally.

He faced the hunching cat and continued growling with his head down, stepping sideways with his hind legs; he put the prune of his nose firmly against Sally, all the while drooling on her, nudging her across the grass. The growls rose in his throat and, as they rose, grew sharper and sharper until he was yelping against Sally's fur.

The cat first purred, a soft bubbling sound; with the weight of the dog's nose on her, the purring became a yowl, long and agonized. As the dog prodded and bumped her with his whole head the yowling turned to a shrill offended wail, harrowingly human in both pitch and attitude.

It was this wailing of Sally's that roused Miss Poole. The pugnacious sounds of the dog, whom she saw as a large unwelcome beast wetting her cat's soft fur with his slippery jowls angered her. It was the sort of intrusion she hated most.

For the moment Miss Poole forgot that it was Heather she was meeting. She was confronted by an unmannered dog; it might as well have been a person, though Miss Poole was usually more charitable with animals. She concentrated on the personality of the dog; she saw nastiness, intrusion, a bulky stranger terrorizing a small well-brushed cat, actually bullying the little thing, a stranger harassing a life-long resident! It infuriated her and, although she had thought of nothing else for the past day, Heather's face – the grinning, overpowdered mask with the silly voice – did not occur to Miss Poole at that moment. The dog was the intruder; the foolish woman did not exist. And Sally, the dear little cat with the bow and bell at her throat . . .

Miss Poole rushed out to the lawn; Sally spun round and leaped into Miss Poole's arms, curled up and squirted urine over her dress. This Miss Poole ignored. She turned to Rufus and shook her finger at him.

'Go away! You leave this poor thing alone, do you hear?' She spoke as if to a delinquent child. 'That's just about enough of that. Now off you go!' Miss Poole stamped on the grass.

Chastened, Rufus pawed a tuft of grass and barked. Holding Sally high and away from him, Miss Poole reached for Rufus's neck-fur to calm him.

'Don't you touch that dog.'

It was Heather; she spoke slowly, pausing after each word, with poison in her voice. She had appeared from an opening in the bougainvillea at the far side of the garden.

Miss Poole straightened. Rufus ran to Heather and let himself be stroked.

'If this dog is yours,' said Miss Poole, 'I would suggest you keep it on a leash. My cats do no [...] take kindly to strange dogs, even less to strange people. Strangers sometimes get scratched, you see.'

They faced each other: Miss Poole with her hair in a bun, in brown tweed darkened with a streak of cat-piss, flat-chested, yellow-grey in complexion with light feline tufts of facial hair, rocking her cat mechanically at her bosom as a mother does a small child; Heather, her blue dress wrinkled at the back from the hot drive, her blonde-streaked hair half-fixed, thick-calved, pudgy with drink, her lips a bright sticky red, a fleshy braceleted arm holding her dog's collar. The cat made her bubbly purr; the dog moaned, tugged forward. In the playing field beyond the trees, the whack of sticks, the fuguing screech of the girls at play; and on the other side of the compound, in the direction of the staff houses, past the bamboo grove to the boggy meadow, the swamp and stream, a racket of noise started up, as it always did just before dusk with almost industrial persistence: frogs scrooped and croaked like rough boards being planed, and hylas and bats squeaked like rusty nails being pounded. It was a vast carpentry shop in the bog beyond the staff houses, where many demon workers hammered and sawed near dusk but, for all the efficient-sounding noise, produced nothing more than a penetrating swamp smell.

'Heather Monkhouse, your new domestic science teacher.'

'Domestic science? The Ministry told me you do English and drama,' Miss Poole said with surprise. 'I teach domestic science and I think the girls have quite enough of that.'

'Well, I was told –'

'You will find, Miss Monkhouse, that in the East

African civil service words mean nothing. People say a lot and do very little. We try to do things differently at this school.'

'I was told I would do needlework.' Heather was insistent.

'But that's impossible.' Miss Poole tried to laugh; she did not succeed; she cleared her throat. 'I do needlework, as well as cookery, mothercraft and flower arrangement. You may help with these, of course, but as far as we're concerned English and drama are your subjects. Some time soon there will be a staff meeting – you are required to attend. We can settle this matter at that time, as well as when you will teach, what your set books will be, and so forth. I like grammarians. I was rather hoping you would be a grammarian –'

'Well, I was told I would do needlework. That's all I know.' Heather tried to be as obtuse as she could.

Miss Poole went on, 'There are other odds and ends of school business. As English mistress you will have the school magazine, and I can tell you'll have to work jolly hard to make it as good as last year's magazine. The Christian Union, of course, the Bible study group which we're all expected to chair once a month – oh, masses of things. It may look a small school, but an enormous great deal is happening in our compound.'

'I don't see any girls,' said Heather, measuring her sarcasm carefully.

'They're at play,' said Miss Poole quickly, 'over there. Fortunately we have a Games Mistress who has charge of them after four. I can't promise you, but you can be reasonably certain of having your evenings free. It's our playtime too, so to speak. But you'll find you'll be well occupied.'

'But how super.'

'I think that will be all for the moment. I should remind you, though I'm told you've been in East Africa several years, um, the unit of time,' now Miss Poole was lecturing, 'the unit of time here is the month, often the year. I don't accept this. I try to make it the minute, minutes are golden. I tell my girls that. I like punctuality.'

'So I've heard.' Heather smiled.

'Rose will show you to your house.' She turned to go, but clucked and added, 'How foolish of me. *I* am Miss Poole.'

Heather muttered a reply and watched her go. When the door to Miss Poole's house banged, Rufus pulled away and trotted to the window. He put his forepaws on the window-sill and howled. Feeling an insect on her elbow, Heather stiffened, held her breath and slapped. Her palm hit the soft bulk of fingers.

There was a cry of pain. Heather turned, saw a figure and immediately took a step backward. The girl was short and wore a ragged ankle-length dress, a sun-faded beret pulled down over her ears and black plastic sunglasses. On her neck, uncovered by the beret, were dirty reddish-gold curls, very tiny and stiff. The girl's face and arms, which Heather first thought were white, were not white but pale and membranous, an eerie translucence which showed pink and blue threads just under the skin-surface. The exposed parts of the girl's body – face, arms, neck, ankles – were blotched and scabbed with violet sores. The girl's features were African: a thick nose, a wide mouth; this mouth was an added ugliness – her thick pale lips hung in a heavy frown of pain.

'I am Rose,' said the girl. She dangled a key-ring in Heather's face.

7
B.J.

'Do you drink?'

'Sure thing.'

'You should do. In a place like this.'

'You just got here, right?'

'A few minutes ago. I left Nairobi this morning.'

'You been in Africa very long?'

'Seven years.'

'You're lucky.'

'*Lucky?* I don't quite understand.'

'If you came out seven years ago, then you were here at the time of Independence. That must have been really exciting.'

'I never noticed.'

'Seven years,' said the girl. 'Golly, I've only been here a little over four months. But the Memsab – that's what we call Miss Poole – she was *born* here, for cry-eye.'

'What part of the States are you from?' asked Heather.

The girl's mouth dropped open. She looked dumbfounded for a few seconds, then began to giggle. 'How in heck,' she said, 'did you know I was from the States?'

'Just a wild guess.'

'Well, for pete's sake,' said the girl, shaking her head and smiling broadly.

The girl had come in while Heather was unpacking; she had said hello and asked if she could help. It was then that Heather asked if she drank. Heather now showed the girl a gin bottle. The girl wagged her finger no; she accepted a warm lime squash. Heather poured an inch of gin into a glass and glanced at the girl: she wore plaid bermuda shorts and a sweatshirt with markings on the front which Heather could not make out; her stockingless feet were in low scuffed sneakers. She was not fat, but would be in a few years. There was a look of deep serenity in her face as she held up her glass of lime squash, sloshed it and stared at the bubbles rising.

'Crazy, isn't it?' She smiled and focused her eyes from the bubbles to Heather.

'What do you mean?'

'I mean,' the girl sloshed the lime again, 'here we are in East Africa, in the boondocks. We're here and everyone else is somewhere else. No, that's not what I mean. What I mean is, we're *no*place and everyone else is *some*place. Get it?'

'You've been to Nairobi?'

'Oh, yeah, Nairobi. Big deal,' said the girl. 'It's like Omaha. Ever been to Omaha?'

'No, but I've always wanted to visit the States –'

'Well, if you go to the States, *don't* go to Omaha. It's really cruddy, let me tell you. Like Nairobi, with lots of farm-types, people eating delicacies with big ugly hands and complaining. My father once ... Hey!' The girl suddenly sat up. Heather noticed that she sat indelicately, knees apart, like a lewd fishwife or a small girl. 'I didn't even tell you my name – it's Bettyjean, only everyone calls me B.J., except the Memsab, who calls everyone Miss this and Miss that. I'm B.J. Lebow.'

'You Americans have such extraordinary names.'

'It's sort of Jewish. It used to be Lebowitz, I guess. You probably knew that, everybody does. But I'm no Jew. I went to Israel one summer. That cured me. What a bunch of boy scouts.'

'The Jews have a tragic history.'

'So do the Africans,' said the girl with a shrug. 'I know your name. Heather Monkhouse. Boy, Heather's a nice name.'

'I'm glad you like it.'

'We only heard you were coming yesterday, but we weren't sure you were arriving today. The Memsab refused to tell us, but we're sure she knew. She doesn't tell us *anything*.'

'No, I supposed not.'

'She's a settler, did I tell you that? At least her father was. I guess she's okay in her way, and all that.'

'Of course.' Heather finished her pink gin and made herself another. As drops of angostura fell slowly into the clear liquid and dispersed in small inverted explosions Heather asked lightly, 'Tell me, B.J., what have they been saying about me?'

B.J. flushed but did not pause. 'Nothing really. Just that you're coming, nobody knew when, and you're doing English and drama. You used to be in Nairobi, I think they said Nairobi, and you're from England etcetera. Nothing really.'

'They haven't been telling tales, have they?' Heather took a long swallow of the gin. 'People in Africa have an incredible knack for saying all sorts of outrageous things.'

'Like?'

'Oh, outrageous nasty things. I can't think of an example at the moment. Yes, I can. There was a widow in Nairobi I knew about. People said she went to bed with her house-boy. Pretty soon, no one would talk to her.'

'That's terrible,' said B.J. with feeling.

'Well, I'm only repeating what I heard. You know how people are.'

'Yeah,' said B.J., 'but suppose it was true. Let's say the

widow *was* sleeping with an African. Is that any reason for not talking to the lady? Africans are people, too. I know the Memsab hates them, being born here like she was, but gee whizz,' she said, pained, 'they're *people*, you know.' B.J. wanted to say more; she muttered and added, 'So many people got this *thing* about black people.'

'Yes, of course,' Heather said. 'But what did people say about, ha-ha, *me*? Did they say anything embarrassing?'

'It all depends what you mean by embarrassing.'

'Look, B.J., you're a big girl, aren't you? I'm asking you quite simply what people have been saying about me. It would make things a lot easier if you came right out and told me. I don't care if it's unpleasant. I just like to know where I stand.'

B.J. looked at Heather with large long-lashed eyes. Her skin was clear, pinkish; she wore no make-up. Her lips were full, teeth perfect.

'Can I call you Heather?'

'By all means.' Heather took another swallow of the gin and braced herself.

'Okay, Heather.' B.J. tilted her head and continued. 'What you're asking me to do is repeat a rumour. I suppose some people might think it's a fair question, it being about you and everything like that. But I don't repeat rumours, not even *to* people about the *same* people. I wouldn't tell you what I heard because it's not fair to you and not fair – maybe you don't agree with this, I don't know – to the people who spread the rumours. What you do is your business, isn't that right? That's the way I look at it. So what do you care what people think about you? Man, I hate this gossip-gossip-gossip, especially here in Africa, you know what I mean?'

'You mean you're not going to tell me what people think of me, what they've been saying.'

'It's not that exactly.'

'It *is* that. Exactly that.' Heather lit a cigarette and huffed and puffed the smoke. She put her fist to her mouth and coughed, then said, 'Well, I don't care.'

'That's the spirit, Heather!' B.J. finished her lime squash.

Heather looked around the room. She said nothing for several minutes, then sighed and looked forlornly at B.J. 'It was awful, wasn't it? You don't have to answer. I didn't even have to ask. I know it was perfectly frightful. People are always saying frightful things about me. There was a particular incident I had in mind –'

'Please don't talk about it. I mean, when people talk about themselves I go all funny inside. I don't know what to say.'

'Try listening,' Heather said sharply. She was angry but realized she had spoken too quickly. The girl was young, she knew absolutely nothing. A typical American face, thought Heather: empty, without a trace of sin on it. Heather knew she had been needlessly sharp. She apologized.

'That's okay,' said B.J. 'You've had a long drive – you must be really tired.'

Jesus, thought Heather. She tried to change the subject. 'What do you think of East Africa? I don't mean Nairobi – I know what you think of that.'

'Africa's the sexiest place in the world,' said B.J. without hesitation.

'Well, that depends on what you know about sex,' said Heather. 'Or the world.'

'It really is.' B.J. grinned.

'What makes you say that?'

'I don't know. But it's sexy, the sun, the grass, all the naked people. It's smelly. It's really wild. Then there are

59

other things, stupid things. Africa,' B.J. said, still smiling, 'I didn't expect it.'

'You knew you were coming –'

'Oh, yeah, I knew I was coming. I read the books and all that stuff. I did my homework,' said B.J. 'But there were things I didn't expect, like all the people in Nairobi getting dressed up. Men have to wear *ties* in the hotels, for criminy sake! And it's a hundred in the shade, not to mention in the African jungle.'

'Nairobi is hardly in the jungle,' said Heather.

'Well, you know what I mean. In Africa. All the yes-bwana, no-bwana. They even have fox-hunting, horse-riding with the velvet hats and red coats, like in the movies, jumping over fences ...' B.J. seemed at a loss and then said, 'Here they are, in Africa of all places, and you see these guys in their crazy suits on horses, trotting through muddy villages blowing horns and shouting *Tally-ho!*'

'I'm sorry you feel that way.' Heather was abrupt. 'Personally I am a most frightful old snob. I am all for the aristocracy. I love to see them around the place, riding their horses, wearing ties, shooting in their tweeds. It's civilized. It's good. It's English, if you know what I mean.'

Her accent had changed, from the slow plea ('People are always saying frightful things about me') a moment earlier to a clipped tonelessness, each hard word frozen and bloodless, definite and confident, almost sneering. The change had come in a matter of minutes.

B.J. recognized the change; it had taken her nearly four months to see, but now she knew what was happening. She had on her arrival thought the English people in Africa to be the friendliest, warmest people on earth: they always inquired about the United States, they showed interest, they conducted conversations with ease and order. But something was missing, politeness maybe; although the inquiries were phrased nicely, the interest seemed like condescension. The order of the nice response in the end was an offence because it was all ready-made, as if contempt, stirred into a soup-mix of dry phrases, was being served up as instant Olde England. It was sad. The English practised and even admired dishonest cleverness. They were people who decided on a pose and, believing none of it, carried it off. In this they showed the greatest uncertainty; it was only playing. As soon as Heather said, 'I am a most frightful old snob' B.J. knew it was a lie and was embarrassed for Heather. If she's only a teacher, then her father's not Lord So-and-so, and if she's like me, what's she got to be snobby about? B.J. thought. And what's so special about the English?

'My room-mate, Pamela Male, she's English,' said B.J. gamely.

'Yes?'

'She's quite interested in meeting you, being English herself.'

'You must bring her around.'

The going was hard. 'Oh, I will,' said B.J. 'You'll like her.'

Heather leaned towards B.J. 'Tell me, what was that perfectly dreadful *thing* that brought me here? That Rose person.' It was a command, not a question.

B.J. looked into her empty glass. 'The poor kid. She's an albino. I think you say alb*ee*no. Funny, I never thought there could be African albinos. But that was stupid of me, wasn't it? If we – you know, white people – if we have albinos, why shouldn't Africans have them, too?'

'Quite.'

'The girls laugh at her. She's quite intelligent, but doesn't see so well. The Memsab took her in. She sort of helps around the place, doing I don't know what exactly. I feel for her, really I do. The sun must kill her. I'll bet she's unhappy.'

'Why should she be unhappy? All Africans want to be white. She's got her wish, hasn't she?' Heather laughed, tilting her head back and holding her throat with one hand.

'You shouldn't joke about things like that.' B.J. spoke slowly. 'How would you like it if you were like that?'

'Don't you see? I *am*. We're all of us albinos in East Africa, aren't we?'

'It's not the same thing.'

Heather relented. 'Suppose not. Bad joke.' She swirled her empty glass, tipped it up and gulped air. 'Well, I really must –'

'Oh, sure,' said B.J. standing brightly. 'Look, Heather, if there's anything at all I can do I'd be glad –'

'No, honestly, I wouldn't hear of it. You've been most kind.' Heather paused. 'Believe me, most kind. You must forgive my rudeness.' The accent was now gone. 'I'm too old to change. Sometimes I'm a horrible bitch. Please take no notice. You're a very sweet girl, B.J.'

'Gee.' B.J. flapped her arms helplessly and started to leave. Then she stopped and turned. 'Oh, *now* I know! I thought you were a good guesser. What an idiot I am!' She pointed to the markings on her sweatshirt which, when she pulled the bottom down, stretched and read *San Jose State College*. 'You *knew* all the time!'

How can someone so stupid get so far from home? Heather tried to put thoughts of B.J. out of her mind, but the image of B.J. remained, sitting awkwardly, knees apart, a lime squash in her hand, correcting Heather, contradicting her sweetly and stupidly. She is innocent, thought Heather, and, yes, I am a bitch. But innocence is a bigger bitchery.

Heather flung her empty glass at the wall. When it hit,

and smashed, a lizard ran out from behind a picture, paused near an unshaded light protruding from the wall, flattened itself and turned white. Heather stared at the lizard for several minutes: it did not alter its colour and, although it was very white, it neither blended with the wall nor moved.

B.J. walked back to her house in the darkness. It was past six, she knew: she could not hear the girls. There was no human sound, only the flutter and intermittent screech of large birds, kites or ravens probably, flapping blindly for a perch, and from the swamp below the gulping rabble of frogs squatting in the murk, a sound which occasionally kept B.J. awake. It was a noise worse than traffic.

B.J. was pretty, she gave off perfumes, but she was dense. Her nerves lived deep in her sweet pink flesh. She had to be touched to be awakened, physically touched. Slapped, she got angry; caressed, she felt desire, and swallowed. The contempt Heather had just uttered perplexed rather than angered her. As she walked through the grass from Heather's house to the one she shared with Pamela Male, B.J. replayed the conversation; she objected to the blunt sounds Heather's words had made and deeply pitied Heather.

The photograph of the Indian child with the swollen belly, picking through Bombay garbage, the spectacular calendar sunset of Kodachrome Yosemite – these caused no quickening of recognition in B.J. She preferred to smell the garbage, swat the flies, hold and cuddle the child; she had to feel the setting sun on her face, roll on the grass, dampen her bermudas with dew. Her denseness (which she was well aware of and pondered) prevented any pictured vision from awakening her. She hated movies and never read with any pleasure unless she either knew the director or author, or had been to the place. One of her reasons for coming to Africa was that she had seen all the films, read all the books; the descriptions and visions interested her (she had a huge catalogue of exotica in her head as a result), but were a long way from giving satisfaction. She wanted more than the two dimensions of pretty pictures, more than the garbled pidgin of kitchen natives. She wanted to touch, smell, *feel* the place deep in her where those nerves lived; she was dying to sink her teeth into a fresh equatorial orange and spray the pips into the tall grass.

She had once explained it to Miss Male: 'I have to plunge right in. Get it?' As a result of this passion for total immersion, which Miss Male saw as specifically American, B.J. had travelled extensively in her twenty-one years. She jetted to foreign places, touched things and smelled her fingers. She had hugged a Doric column on the Acropolis and stared straight up its pock-marked shaft to the blue Greek sky; she had put her hands into the Ganges where saddhus bathed, kissed the Blarney Stone, peeled a banana in Caracas, rubbed her cheek against the Vatican. It provided simple useful information, but revealed no secrets. It was her way of knowing the world, the child's way, an international show and tell.

Her father indulged her, urged her on: 'Look at B.J., Mother. Now she wants to ride that mangy old camel!'

In Hong Kong, aged fifteen, she had sampled rat.

'You're not really gonna *eat* those awful things?'

'I want to see what they *taste* like,' said B.J. playfully. She had dysentery for a week. But B.J. could not help it. She knew she was dense, but was also curious, a wondering that was at times harmful, for no second-hand description, no matter how detailed, could satisfy it. It was this wondering insulated in layers of density that had led her to join the Peace Corps and come to Africa. For once, she was travelling alone; as her father said, she was a big girl now and would have to learn to find out things for herself.

A flashlight bobbed towards her. Miss Male.

'Is she here?'

'Who?' asked B.J. She had been thinking about peanut butter. She often thought of peanut butter. It seemed the one thing you could not get in East Africa, in spite of the gigantic peanut crop.

'The Mother of the Year,' said Miss Male.

'I wish you wouldn't call her that, Pam.'

'I thought you Americans liked that sort of thing.'

'Well, we do and we don't –'

'For heaven's sake, B.J., is she here or not?'

'If you mean Heather Monkhouse – yes, she's here. She's very sad.'

'I daresay she's got bags of things to be sad about.' Miss Male laughed and aimed her flashlight at Heather's house.

'Be kind to her,' said B.J. 'I told her you were dying to meet her, you being English.'

'You're a dear,' said Miss Male. 'Oh, by the way, you've got a caller. That chap from the Electricity Board. I'm off to the Staff Room – see you anon.'

'So long, Pam.'

A very short African in a dark suit scrambled to his feet when B.J. entered her house. The African breathed out, but said nothing; he wrung his hands and grinned.

'*Habari gani*, Wangi,' said B.J. cheerfully.

'*Mzuri.*' He tugged at his tie.

'My God, sit *down*. You Africans got better manners than the so-called English people around here!'

8
Wangi

'Boy, have *you* been brainwashed,' said B.J.

Wangi had come for tea.

'I mean, I thought only English people drank tea.'

'As you know,' said Wangi, 'the British were our masters.' He held his saucer in the air and, pursing his lips, stirred the tea with a rapid rotary motion of the spoon.

'You poor thing,' said B.J., screwing up one eye to show she was really sorry.

Wangi smiled as if he had scored a point. He made no reply, only stared. The staring was something B.J. had never liked about Africans; that, with a dark silence. They seemed to gape at her endlessly, their eyes flashing from her feet to her head, lingering on knees, arms, and breasts, without a word. She had been told that Africans loved to talk and tell long stories in front of the fire, or anywhere, which was why they had an oral history, nothing written down: talking was their real gift. They would walk miles to shoot the bull, that was how B.J. imagined it. And several of the lectures in her Peace Corps training said what chatterboxes Africans were and how they loved to pull your leg.

That's what they said. But B.J. had not seen Africans do anything of the kind. They entered a room and produced agonizing silences by gazing watery-eyed at everything. One of these long silences, the African scrutinizing fabric and flesh, seemed to destroy conversation. Worse than this, she found that she could not sit still under the large eyes that never seemed to meet her own, eyes that fixed themselves (as Wangi's were at that moment) on her breasts and flashed from one to the other. B.J. poured more tea into Wangi's cup. Wangi stared first at the bulging *San* then the bulging *Jose*. She returned to her chair and, for no reason at all, giggled.

B.J. had been certain almost from the first that she did not like Africans very much. Their staring, their silence, their odd humour and poor English – all these taken into consideration with the great strength obvious under their lapels made them seem mysterious. They were not necessarily dangerous, but they possessed a secret B.J. had not yet learned.

At first she had assumed Africans were like American Negroes. But she was not really sure what Negroes were like. Her father distrusted Negroes and told B.J. to distrust them too: 'If you take one home you'll be breaking your Daddy's heart, and your Daddy loves you, remember.' B.J. admired her father's honesty nearly as much as she detested his sentiment. But it was understandable: he had been born in Pine Bluffs, orphaned at eleven, raised by relatives and educated haphazardly in Chicago. He had taken a number of menial jobs, waiting on table, lugging moulds in a tyre factory, cleaning spittoons; he had earned enough money to go to college. He loved to talk about the degrading jobs he had done; that his whole family had been illiterate and he had scrubbed spittoons were two of his greatest sources of pride.

Very late in life, bald with worry and eaten by a stomach ulcer, her father became a dentist. He married, moved to San Diego and in twenty-one years earned enough money so that he could swear that his kids would never have the rotten hardships he had; they'd have everything he'd never had. B.J. had once pressed him for reasons why he disliked Negroes. He began by describing his past, how his life had been as hard as any schwarz's; as he spoke, his words became more and more crude and finally shifted to a tirade of racial abuse so pointlessly vulgar, from someone B.J. thought of as the gentlest man in the world, that she resolved never to challenge him again on the race question and to date, in private, as many Negroes as she could.

She looked, but saw none, and had to settle for foreign students. She ran into them all over the campus: Jamaicans, Filipinos, Koreans, Thais, Nigerians, Indians in saris, Hungarians with scraggly beards who had thrown rocks at Soviet tanks, and dozens of other nationalities. All the foreign students sat together in the Student Union, at the same table, exchanging heavily accented platitudes. For a reason B.J. remained clueless about, every one of them was studying agricultural economics. The foreign students were easy to meet; they hungered for companionship. The slightest word of greeting roused them to stand, bow graciously and offer a cup of coffee. They taught B.J. their proverbs, how to say hello and how-are-you in the popping labials of their vernaculars; they reminisced about their countries, which they said were nice and green and poor. They were sick with loneliness; when they walked down the college corridors they were jostled, for they were dark undersized people in a land of white giants. After classes they gathered pathetically at their sticky table in the Union. For B.J. the foreign students were all San Jose could claim of the exotic. Also they were coloured, some of them in more ways than Negroes.

But there were no Negroes at the college and B.J. lived in the wrong neighbourhood for Negroes to be easily accessible. She lamented this: there was a certain something she liked about them, she never knew what, maybe their tremendous vim.

Wangi had been staring (B.J. checked her watch) nearly fifteen minutes. She had never known him to be so engrossed with her body; but, then, she had not known Wangi very long. A week previously she had met him at a party at the home of his cousin, the District Education Officer, Wilbur something, who had just been transferred from Nairobi. Wangi had what seemed to be a good job with the Electricity Board and dressed in dark suits, his shoes always shined. He used after-shave lotion and was scrubbed to the point of being polished. His snazzy appearance had been something of a disappointment for B.J., who expected skins, but sitting there in her living-room he seemed to her like a crouching Congolese figurine, hard, glossy, black, representing something. B.J. could stand his silence no longer. In desperation she said, 'Tell me something about yourself.'

'My cousin is the District Education Officer.'

'You *told* me that already. Anyway I knew it. Tell me something else,' B.J. urged.

'I did my primary education in Nairobi.'

'I *know* that, silly. But what about before then – what about your village and like that?'

'My village is poor.'

'I'll bet,' B.J. clucked.

Wangi peered at her. 'Do you know,' he said, 'I didn't have a pair of shoes until I was twenty.'

'What a shame! Cripe, I've had shoes my whole life.'

'Village life is terrible,' sighed Wangi. 'That's why we killed the British. We had to. They wanted us to live in villages.'

'People still live in villages, don't they?'

'*I* don't,' said Wangi. 'The British are terrible. They hate you and they don't say it, but you know they hate you. It's terrible. You never know if they hate you, but you know if they're British they have to. That's the way the British are. So we killed them.'

'Were you in those gangs?'

'Oh, yes.'

'Wow,' said B.J. softly.

'No,' said Wangi, 'two of them: Mau-Mau.'

'You don't mean you actually . . .' B.J. swallowed, wondering whether to ask. 'You actually . . . ah . . . killed –'

'Oh, yes,' Wangi said, brightening. 'Everyone had to. That's how you get free. It's not easy. They used to call us natives and what-not –'

'Sure, but a native just means someone who lives in a particular –'

'That's what I used to hate, when they said "You bloody natives". So I didn't mind joining up, and one night,' Wangi continued, interspersing his story with little bursts of laughter, 'we went to a farm in Nyeri District. My uncle said that now we ha-ha just have to do this. These buggers have been ha-ha treating us too badly. I took my knife ha-ha and was creeping slowly ha-ha –'

'Please, Wangi. Tell me about your village.'

'Don't you want to hear the story? It's very interesting.'

'Tell me about your village. I'll bet it's great.'

'That's interesting too. I'll take you there some day. You can meet my father and his wives.'

'Wives? More than one?'

'Three,' said Wangi. 'He has more than twenty children.'

'Twenty! Goodness, no wonder you were poor!'

Wangi looked confused. 'No,' he said, 'children are good. Children didn't make us poor. The British did.'

B.J. was not sure what she should say. She knew that if she talked about the British she would be betraying Miss Poole and Heather. As much as they got on her nerves, still she could not bring herself to talk behind their backs. She noticed Wangi had started staring again. She began to think that perhaps village life was not so bad. But she had no way of telling, about that or poverty, and for a moment the thought crossed her mind that her children would have all the things she never had: misery, hardship, poverty, dirty jobs. She would not give them a thing. It would do them a lot of good.

'That's why we like you Americans,' Wangi said finally, his gaze resting on B.J.'s bare knee. 'You're kind people. You talk to us. You even like us, don't you?'

'Of course we do,' said B.J. She was glad of a chance to say it, but as soon as she did she had a feeling Wangi would be a regular visitor. She was not troubled by this; she knew she would go out with him. There were many reasons, a little bit of politics, maybe some guilt, and even if there were no love there would be sympathy and curiosity. He wasn't a bad guy. And even if he was (but he wasn't) life at the school was dull and why else had she gone all the way into Los Angeles to take the Peace Corps exam and put up with the Mickey Mouse of three months' training and come all the long way to Africa, if not to get to know Africans?

9
Rose

Crouched simian-fashion in the dark hollows of a giant bougainvillea in the garden, Rose looked across the compound to the girls' dormitories. The buildings were lighted, but to Rose's scorched eyes the lights were fogged faintly-luminous haloes, like bulbs underwater. They began to go out.

She waited until there was complete darkness and then crept towards the kitchen door where a small light burned; she saw it only as a small glow, no bigger than a fire-fly. It illuminated nothing for her, but she did not need it to find her way. As soon as she tapped on the door the glow was gone. A key clicked inside. The door creaked open an inch. Rose pushed the door open, making the hinges snarl, and felt her way through the kitchen, sniffing the familiar odours: bread, dust, soap, oranges, mangoes, flour, all permeated with the sharp stink of cat-piss. Ahead of her she heard slow steps, but there was no voice, no other sound. She saw nothing. She slid her bruised hand along the edge of the sideboard, touched at the jamb of the door and entered the living-room. Now the softness of the rug under her bare feet, a small table brushing her thigh and, across the room, the large front window, all she could see, blurred round in the white glow of the moon.

She had not removed her dark glasses. She moved bent-over, with agility, to a stool she could not see but whose place she was familiar with. The moon did not relieve the darkness for Rose. Like those fish that live deep in the ocean and glow, she had lived her whole life in darkness and gave off a similar pearly light. The dark glasses kept the sun out of her eyes, but she did not wear them to protect her eyes; the glasses were an opaque mask to prevent others from seeing the pink blistered slits beneath. She removed them only when she slept.

She touched the stool and sat, in her ears the slow rhythmic purring of the slumbering cats and the breathing of another person.

'*Nataka chai*, Rose?' asked Miss Poole softly. 'Do you want tea?' The Swahili was delivered with an English intonation, unaccented, the lips scarcely parted.

'Thank you, no.'

'*Iko hapa*,' said Miss Poole. '*Hapana iko njaa?*'

'Little bit,' whispered Rose, again in English.

'*Kitu gani*, Rose?' Miss Poole's voice was impatient. 'What's wrong?'

Rose paused and then said, 'I like talk Englis, madam.' She breathed heavily and nothing more was said in the room for several minutes. The darkness purred with cats. Rose was still; for a second the shiny plastic of her dark glasses caught a moonbeam from the window. The skin that in bright sunlight showed horrible mottle, dead blotches and threads of blood, in the moonlight seemed perfectly white and clear, a radiance Miss Poole loved.

'My poor Rose,' Miss Poole said in English, 'you are night-blooming.'

'Englis,' said Rose, satisfied. She bent forward and hugged her knees; on the stool, her profile forward, skin gleaming, she could have been a newly carved gargoyle about to be hoisted into position on the parapet of a cathedral. Now she spoke in Swahili: 'Yes, I will have tea.'

'Ah,' sighed Miss Poole. There was the clink of the spout

against the cup, the *shuff* of the sugar being spooned from a bowl, three scoops; the cup tinkling on the saucer as it was placed on the floor. 'Here is good tea,' said Miss Poole in Swahili.

When Rose had lifted the cup and sipped, Miss Poole spoke again in Swahili. Rose replied. They continued this way: the dull tongue-flaps of Rose, the English consonants and open Bantu vowels which Miss Poole timidly voiced in low flat tones.

'With the American you say?'

'With the American.'

'For how long?'

'Less than one hour.'

'They talked?'

'Indeed.'

'As friends?'

'No.'

'How do you know?'

'Their voices were different. The new teacher was angry a little bit.'

'Why was she angry?'

'I don't know.'

'Did they talk about me?'

'Your name once. That was all.'

'They drank of course.'

'The American drank lime squash. The other *enguli*.'

'Is there anything else you remember well?'

In broken sentences, with many hesitations, Rose told of the glass being thrown against the wall. She hissed, simulating the smash and finished with, '*Pole*.'

Miss Poole was silent except for her angry breathing.

'Sorry,' said Rose, this time in English.

'And what did you see at the American's house?' asked Miss Poole in Swahili.

10

Carving a Joint

A week later, Miss Poole prayed: 'Our Father, we thank Thee for this delicious repast in full knowledge that there are those of our brethren who have naught. For our daily bread accept our praise and hear our prayer. By Thee all living souls are fed; Thy bounty and Thy loving care with all Thy children let us share. Make us obedient, kind and true, and Grant us strength, O Lord, to be grateful that we may serve Thee. Amen.'

'Amen,' said B.J. and Miss Male.

'And what,' asked Heather, reaching for the potatoes, 'do you plan to serve Him?'

'I beg your pardon, Miss Monkhouse.' Miss Poole jerked her head at Heather. She gave Heather's name a queer pronunciation, as if she were saying 'Mongoose'.

'You said we're . . .' Heather paused and glanced around the table. 'You said we're going to *serve* Him, ha-ha.' She dropped a potato on her plate with a stiff *bonk* and passed the dish.

No one moved to grasp the dish. Heather put it down beside her plate and folded her hands. The expressions on the faces of the women did not change. The women were motionless in intense postures, as if being sketched.

Miss Poole appeared calm. Only her hands, clasping the edge of the table, betrayed her rage. Her knuckles had gone white. When she spoke it seemed as if at any moment her voice would become a scream. 'That is blasphemy, Miss

Monkhouse. This is a Christian school. *We* are Christians. I must ask you to apologize or leave the table.'

Heather nibbled at her lip. She stared at her plate, then looked up and, still expressionless, winked at B.J. and Miss Male, and said, 'I'm terribly sorry. I am a perfect fool, aren't I?'

There was another silence, this one timed, precise. The three women looked at Miss Poole or, rather, at Miss Poole's knuckles which had drained completely of blood and were turning a grey-blue, like ten agates. The food steamed untouched on the table; two moths staggered through the air and made for the light, which hung over the food on a thick fly-specked cord.

'Gee,' a voice began. Everyone turned towards B.J. The words tumbled out with a cheerful clatter that broke the silence like a lawnmower. 'I know this doesn't have anything to do with what we're talking about ... I mean, see, I'm not a Christian, really. I'm a Jew. That is, my father's Jewish, a sort of conservative – I'm a reformed ... So ...' B.J. paused. There was no response. 'I just thought I'd tell you all that because you, ah, Miss Poole, you said we're all Christians and, ah, that's not really, ah, actually ...' B.J.'s voice trailed off. When her voice had gone completely she filled her mouth with bread.

Miss Poole switched off her glare and moved slightly. Miss Male coughed nervously; she saw that Miss Poole was looking at her. In a low defeated voice Miss Poole said, 'Here you are, Miss Male. As our only biologist I'm sure you know more about these things than we do. I'm afraid it's none too sharp, but do your best.' She handed Miss Male a carving knife.

'Thank you,' said Miss Male solemnly. The joint, a sad-looking log that had fat stitched on it with white sodden string, was passed to Miss Male. She examined it with the tines of a long serving fork, said, 'Here goes' and began sawing off large frayed chunks of juiceless meat.

The knife-blade was dull; it cut only because it was chipped in enough places for it to be saw-toothed, jagged. Miss Poole kept the knife dull on purpose, thinking that it would cut less meat from the joint if it were dull and leave more meat for the cats. In fact, the blade was only good for crudely sawing and hacking off pieces; consequently, Miss Poole's knife, because it was dull as a hoe, produced only large pieces. Miss Male cut incautiously. She had discovered, a short time before, Miss Poole's reason for keeping the knife dull. The table shook, the plates rattled as Miss Male sawed at the hard log of burned meat.

'You look like you're trying to kill it, Pam!' said B.J., bright-eyed.

Miss Poole gazed sadly at the mutilated joint and said, 'I think that will be just fine. You may pass the platter around.' When the meat was passed to Miss Poole, she said in a voice that had become suddenly gentle, 'Oh, there's a *delicious* one, and another one. Can you eat all that? You're a little piggy, aren't you? *More?* All right, but just one ...' She forked hunks of meat into her lap, then put her fork on the table. As she did, there was a deep satisfied purr from her lap, where Sally was curled, her head stuck into a plate, licking at meat. Miss Poole removed the plate and placed it on the floor beside her chair. Sally followed, hitting the floor with a thump.

'I sure feel sorry for vegetarians,' said B.J., chewing her meat enthusiastically.

No one heard B.J. or replied; Miss Male and Heather were still watching the little scene at the head of the table; Miss Poole's eyes were on Sally lapping the meat and switching her big tail back and forth.

'Ooo, you're a *fat* pussycat,' said Miss Poole.

When Sally finished, Miss Poole tinkled a little bell; Julius, Miss Poole's aged cook, appeared at the door to the kitchen. Excusing himself in Swahili, he creaked over and took Sally's empty plate and, holding the plate in the air on the pedestal of five long fingers, went back to the kitchen.

B.J. was still chewing. 'Say, speaking of vegetarians, that reminds me – where's Miss Verjee? Couldn't she come?'

'I take it Miss Verjee is the Games Mistress,' said Heather to Miss Male.

'That's right,' said Miss Male. 'The Indian chap.'

Miss Poole spoke with caution. 'Miss Verjee is quite happy where she is.'

'Well, that's what I was wondering,' said B.J. 'Where is she?'

'At her quarters, one would presume,' said Heather.

'No,' said Miss Poole. 'She is a member of staff and, like us all, has duties to perform. At the moment she is refereeing the netball match over at the playing field. She'll see the girls to their dormitories after evening meal.'

'While we're here?'

'What's wrong with that, B.J.?' asked Heather.

B.J. put down her knife and fork. 'You mean to say it doesn't bother you that while you're sitting here eating, Miss Verjee is over there on duty, working like a dog?'

'Interesting simile,' said Heather slicing her meat. She chewed, swallowed and added, 'If she wasn't invited here, then why should *you* get upset about it?'

'It doesn't seem fair,' said B.J. 'Anyway, what gives you the idea I'm upset? I'm not upset. I'm just –'

'Someone has to watch the girls until lights-out,' said

Miss Poole, opening her mouth very wide and then closing it on a forkful of stringy meat.

'Why is the *someone* always Fatima Amirlal Verjee, is all I'm saying.'

'You *do* have a gift for these difficult Asian names,' said Miss Poole, working her jaws on the wad of meat-sinew.

'I think B.J. has a point,' said Miss Male.

'I don't see any point at all,' said Heather.

'The point,' said B.J., facing Heather, 'is I've never seen her in this house. And she works here, is the point.'

'Now really,' fluttered Miss Poole, 'I fail to see what the argument is. Miss Verjee is doing her job. Each of us does her job, only we never seem to be doing our jobs when Miss Verjee is doing hers. Let's not make an issue of it. I know *I* shan't say any more about it.'

'But we're here stuffing ourselves and she's there working, the poor kid.'

All had stopped eating; in the silence that followed B.J.'s words, all the women except Heather resumed. B.J. poked at peas. Heather was still looking at B.J.

'Why is it,' inquired Heather, 'that Americans hate to see people happy? Americans act as if it's a horrible old *sin* for people to enjoy themselves.'

'That's not entirely true,' said Miss Male. 'We English –'

'Let me finish,' said Heather sharply. 'We're here eating and for all I know enjoying ourselves. Miss Verjee isn't here – she's working, in point of fact. But immediately our American friend detects Miss Verjee's absence she decides there's something sinister in it. I do believe she thinks it's racial prejudice.'

'That's absurd,' said Miss Poole. 'How could it be racial prejudice? We're all of us educated women, aren't we? We can have anyone we want in our house – that's not racial prejudice, it's the privilege of the house-owner. I know some people say that we're racially prejudiced, but my answer to them is, if I were racially prejudiced wouldn't I be living in Australia or some white country instead of Africa? I should think so, but we are here, in a black country. There are black faces everywhere –'

'Except at this table,' said B.J. in a whisper.

Heather leaned towards Miss Poole and said with sincerity, 'You're absolutely right.'

Miss Poole's eyes widened at Heather, stunned.

'It's these Americans that come here,' Heather went on, 'that's the only problem with East Africa. It's incredible. What does a Yank know about the lower classes and peasants? We English know they're different, but these Yanks – it really irks me – they think every bod in the world from top to bottom is the same. It's fantastic. Give every nig-nog from here to Kingdom Come some Coca-Cola, peanut butter, corn flakes, comic books, hamburgers, and the whole world will be all right.' Heather paused, screwed up her face and said in what was intended to be an American accent, '*No more prahblims!*' She laughed. 'It's fantastic. You act as if you have no problems in the States – that's what's really fantastic about Yanks. There are poor people in the good old USA, aren't there? You're bloody right, there are! I read somewhere that one-third of the people in the States live in hovels and wear rags, but *no*, you don't stay there and put things right – you come *here* and play the good sheriff, fighting for people's non-existent rights and all that rubbish. And what about your own nig-nogs? I once read –'

'I think you're being a bit unfair,' said Miss Male, folding and unfolding her napkin.

'Well, there's something in what Miss Monkhouse is saying,' said Miss Poole. Again she said 'Mongoose'; it had not been a slip of the tongue the first two times. 'Racial prejudice is jolly difficult to define.'

B.J. looked first at Miss Poole, then at Heather. She spoke, shifting her gaze from one to the other. 'I know Americans aren't perfect. I never said we were. I know poverty's a big hang-up for lots of people. But that's not what we're talking about. At least I'm not. I'm talking about Miss Verjee who isn't here because she's an Indian. She eats with her hands and licks her fingers and her English is bad and things like that. Africans don't like Indians, neither do white people. We all know that, so why don't we just come out and say it, huh?'

'I told you,' said Heather, scraping her loose food together in a little heap with the side of her fork, 'you can't stand to see people enjoying themselves. You always have to ruin it with your bloody self-righteousness.'

'Does anyone want more meat or vegetables?' asked Miss Poole loudly. 'If not, I'll give them to the cats.'

Heather was breathless, B.J. angry, Miss Male hurt and confused. No one replied to Miss Poole and so all the dishes of food were placed on the floor for the cats. B.J.'s downcast eyes caught the swarming cats, fighting for the food, licking the plates with their small pink tongues, plates that she would herself eat from when she came again.

Miss Male cleared her throat. 'How are you finding it here?' she asked Heather.

'Frightful, perfectly frightful,' said Heather. She lit a cigarette and looked at the light-bulb over the table. 'I had forgotten how terrible it is to be among women. It's nothing personal against you chaps, except that you're not men. They say men are bad – and that's true of course, men can be bloody awful. But there's nothing worse than a bunch of women together. It must be our predatory instincts or somesuch. We're all so damned blood-thirsty, we women. When I read in the papers about some bloke murdering his wife I say to myself, "I'll bet it was her own fault". In a group men are pretty jolly, but we're like some breed of ghastly bird, always pecking and clawing –'

Miss Poole had gripped the table-edge, but kept her eyes hard on Heather.

Heather glanced at Miss Poole, saw the knuckles whitening and said quickly, 'I'm sure I'll adjust to it. It takes time, doesn't it?'

'I must say it doesn't take much adjusting to live here in the *bundu*. I rather prefer life here to that awful Nairobi,' said Miss Poole.

Heather threw her head back and gave a stage laugh, loud and brief; Miss Poole was still talking, not to Heather, but to Miss Male.

'– The Africans here are really quite sweet, don't you think so? I find the Africans in Nairobi rather aggressive – bullies, to be frank.'

'Quite,' said Miss Male uneasily. She could add nothing more. Miss Male had been only three months in East Africa. She preferred not to talk about Africans; she usually said that she had nothing against them.

'I've never heard such a thing,' said Heather, exasperated. 'When I was in Nairobi I took no notice of the blacks. I thought they were all the same. Now I see there are differences, those chaps in Nairobi had something after all. They're cheeky, I suppose – that's what we get for spoonfeeding them – but they know how to dress. Not like the *watu* here, dashing about in rags and stinking to high heaven. The typist in our school was a keen little chappie, always neat.' Heather looked at Miss Poole and shook her head from side to side. 'You prefer life here, you say. I don't. These people . . . *smell*. Full stop.'

'To you they small,' B.J. broke in. 'I read somewhere that black people consider whites very unclean because we don't bathe in running water.'

'Isn't it the Indians who feel that way,' said Miss Male, 'not the Africans?'

'Back to Miss Verjee,' said Heather disgustedly.

'Well, Africans *are* very clean,' said B.J.

'You're sure of that?' asked Miss Poole.

'Sure I am.'

'Well, I know I'm hardly an authority –'

'You see, I read somewhere that Africans are very careful about washing. They wash every day,' said B.J.

Heather laughed, again too loudly. 'That's rubbish. I'll bet it was written by a Yank.'

'Of course, Julius may be an exception,' said Miss Poole.

B.J. was silent.

Miss Poole seemed agitated. Sally had crept back on to her lap, and Miss Poole calmed herself by stroking Sally's fur. Now there was silence all around. Miss Poole continued to stroke the cat, saying, 'I've heard all this before a thousand times. Do they wash, don't they wash? Who is cheeky and who isn't. This doesn't make a particle of difference. I said I prefer life here and I mean it. I can handle my Africans – they don't mind if one is firm as long as one is fair. The Africans here are reasonably honest. They have the tribe and the chief. They are living with their own people. Even the English and the Americans go a bit mad when they're away from their own people, there's no denying that.' Miss Poole glanced at B.J. and then continued. 'The Africans lie of course, and steal little things. That's their way. I know Julius is constantly in the sugar, but he doesn't take much, and he does an honest job of work. But I get perfectly ill when I think of those people in Nairobi driving around in their long American cars, having their fiddles at the Maize Marketing Board, spending our hard-earned tax money –'

'I beg your pardon,' said Heather haughtily. 'While these people sit in the mud and beat their bongos, the Africans in Nairobi show a bit of initiative –'

'It's bribery and corruption and you know it,' said Miss Poole matter-of-factly.

B.J. looked at Miss Male, who stared straight ahead, at nothing. She hoped Miss Male would say something. She was English and, in B.J.'s eyes, had a right to speak. In the course of the meal B.J. had heard her own voice; she knew it sounded foolish and American and unlike the other refined, correct English ones at the table; but she could not speak differently. If she said something they would laugh; she had become acutely aware, with an awareness that dumbed her, that she pronounced her *t*'s like *d*'s, as in 'running wadder' and 'Miss Verjee's on doody' (Howdy Doody, thought B.J., grimly: what a stupe I am).

'I grew up with these people,' Miss Poole was saying. 'I know them. They don't belong in big strange cities where all manner of horrible things can happen to them. They need their tribe, the air, the sun –'

'They need to be bloody-minded, that's all. But mind you,' Heather said, dithering, 'I wouldn't give you a shilling for the lot of them. If I had my choice –'

'In Nairobi they are immoral. Drunkards. It's shocking,' said Miss Poole.

'I don't even *care* about Africans. It's fantastic. I don't know why I'm talking like this, but since coming up-country a week ago I've seen nothing but lazy *watu* sitting under trees doing damn-all.'

'There is goodness in them. What would *you* know about that? Yes,' said Miss Poole, with tears in her eyes, 'still some goodness –'

'That's rubbish! Now you sound like an American.' Heather's voice sweetened. 'How does it go? I remember a man in Nairobi telling me, "In East Africa the birds have no song, the flowers have no fragrance, the women have no virtue." So true.'

Heather looked around the table for a reaction. There was only an offended silence. She went on placidly, 'Goodness? *Here?* Not bloody likely, I'd say. I recall a white woman, as white as any of us, was killed by an African not far from where we're sitting. That was a few years ago. She was also, they say,' she paused for effect, 'molested in the most savage way.'

Miss Male looked worriedly at Heather. 'Did it happen here at the school?'

'Oh,' said Heather lightly, '*somewhere* near here. Strangled with her own brassiere, they say. Among other things.'

'Did they catch him?' Miss Male seemed oblivious of the others. Her hand touched at her throat.

'I suppose not, I forget. But it's something to think about, isn't it? Especially when you use big words like goodness and suchlike.'

B.J. stiffened. 'Well, how would you like it if someone spit at you and called you names, like the British did to the Africans here? Yeah,' said B.J., 'and made you live in a village and treated you like dirt. *You* wouldn't like it.'

'I neglected to mention,' said Heather. 'This was *after* Independence. The blacks were in power.'

'Some people have long memories,' said B.J. quickly. On the word *people* she spat a small bubble of spittle into Heather's face.

'Some people possibly,' said Heather, wiping at the spittle. 'Not these people.'

'You didn't –'

'No. They're savages, pure and simple. When you realize that, as I did – and I was just like you, B.J., when I arrived, full of idealism and let's give the chaps a fair chance – when you realize that, you're content and you stop fighting people's battles for them. You wait and see. You'll change.'

'You didn't answer my question,' said B.J. 'How would you like it –'

Heather whipped around and looked B.J. full in the face. 'How would you like it if someone called you a dirty Jew? Would you wrap your bra around his neck and strangle him? *Would you?*'

'It's not quite the same thing,' said Miss Male attempting to calm Heather. 'Anti-semitism is hardly –'

'It's close,' said Heather. 'It's ruddy close. Human life means nothing here. I lock my doors here, I can tell you that. Who knows, some dirty great spade might take it into his head –'

Miss Poole scraped her chair back; she was trembling with suppressed rage. She helped Sally to the floor. Sally yowled while Miss Poole swayed cobra-like at Heather and said, 'My Africans can be trusted, they work hard, they respect me. My Africans ... my Africans are better than your Africans.'

She did not speak loudly but she spoke with conviction, her voice steady, even if her body was not. When she finished Heather opened her mouth to say something, but she had only said one word when from the kitchen there was a terrific crash which sent all the cats, led by Sally, looping over chairs and into the bedroom. The crash did not end at once; it tapered off with the splinter, shatter and tinkle of glass. Heather said nothing more; Miss Poole jumped up and ran to the kitchen. As soon as the door flapped shut, Heather's lips curled slowly into a smile.

Now they sat in the living-room, holding coffee cups on their laps. They spoke politely in turn, their voices growing softer and softer. Julius had dropped the chocolate *mousse* and had broken Miss Poole's heavy crystal bowl. His penitent sighing, as he mopped the pieces of glass on the floor, was audible even in the living-room. Neither the dessert nor the breakage was mentioned by any of the women.

'Fruit?' asked Miss Poole coldly.

B.J. said she would like a banana, but she had no sooner said it than she realized she had mispronounced it, given it a short *a*. To make matters worse she added, 'As we say back home.'

Miss Male's head was in her hands. The cats had returned from the bedroom and were squabbling for room on Miss Poole's narrow lap. When B.J. finished her banana she looked for a place to put the large damp peel; seeing no receptacle, she cradled it in her hands. She felt bites on her legs. There were cat fleas in her chair; she dangled the banana peel by its hard tip and with her free hand rubbed her thighs and calves, squashing the grey fleas and leaving small streaks of juice on her skin.

Their talking had now stopped altogether; the only sounds came from outside the room – frogs, whining locusts, bats; bugs pattered on the screened windows. Heather puffed her cigarette and, expelling the smoke loudly to get everyone's attention, glanced around the room.

'I know what you're all thinking,' she said. 'But as bad as we are – and I *know* we're bad; I don't need Americans to tell me that – we're the best they'll ever get. Who wants to live in Africa, what white people? Only cranks, fools, failures ...'

Before anyone could respond, Heather said again, 'We're the best they'll get. The best,' she added almost with malice.

11
Games

Heather knew she had talked too much at Miss Poole's, and hated herself for having spoken sincerely; she felt she had given them a chance to know her doubt. She regretted the evening. Strangers had called out to her from a distance; their indistinct intentions and her own loneliness had eased her into their company, but only when she was near did she recognize them as strangers. They had duped her and looted her of her sincerity. It was not new to her and this made her feel worse. There was a further humiliation: they had watched her; they would be next to her for a whole term, reminding her of this loss.

Miss Poole, because she seemed pathetic, had won. Where there were sentimental witnesses the old, the ugly and the inept always came out best. On leaving Miss Poole's house, Heather resolved that she would not say another word socially to her again. But there were several other things to consider: another humiliating defeat, sourly sitting in her throat; there was the fact that an invitation had been extended and she had accepted. The invitation would have to be returned; the school was too small and tightly balanced for safe rituals to falter into irregularity; chaos would follow. The week after Miss Poole's dinner, Heather handed a note to her cook and told him to take it to the Memsab and to wait for a reply. Miss Poole initialled the note and the next day joined B.J. and Miss Male at Heather's house for a meal. That evening Miss

Male invited Heather and Miss Poole for a meal with her and B.J. And so it went, in rotation, with all the women always present; a pattern had formed. Attendance at the weekly dinners was obligatory, for this was the bush; with the exception of the Horse and Hunter, a rustic hotel fifteen miles up the road, there was nowhere else to go, nothing else to do. They were all unmarried white women, living together in a remote post, in a black country. In the absence of privacy lay their safety; an assertion of privacy by any of them would have meant threat. Even if B.J. and Miss Male had not yet caught on, they would soon realize this necessity as, in her five years, Heather had. There could be no excuse for not playing along with the others.

With sadness Heather sent the second invitation to Miss Poole. She knew the drill: the dinner would start with a 'sundowner' at four when the girls went out to the playing field, and would continue through the evening, moving from the veranda to the sitting-room to the dining-room and then back to the veranda for the last drink. Heather hated the idea of the intrusion, inescapable, possibly humiliating. But after getting the initialled invitation back, she realized that Miss Poole was similarly inconvenienced and maybe even annoyed by the fraudulent gesture of hospitality. When Heather considered it she grew absolutely pleased to be giving the second dinner; she could get back at Miss Poole and, if everything went well, she could do what she wanted to the hag at the head of the table who had served burned meat and said, 'My Africans are better than your Africans.'

Miss Poole arrived at Heather's on time.

'I wasn't sure you were coming,' said Heather blandly. 'I couldn't make out your initials on the note. Did you use a quill?'

Rufus barked, interrupting Miss Poole's reply, but when Miss Poole took her place on the veranda she spoke to Rufus softly, scratched behind his ear and even fearlessly held his lower jaw while she examined his teeth; the dog wagged his tail, grunted and flopped beside her.

'He has a spot of caries,' said Miss Poole.

'It must be this poxy place,' said Heather.

'Hi, all!' called B.J. from the grass. Miss Male was next to her. B.J. held something in her hands; one hand was clasped over the other. 'We got a hurt bug here. I hope you have a first-aid kit.'

'Drink?' asked Heather, ignoring B.J.

Miss Poole asked for sherry, the others beer. When it was brought B.J. opened her hands a crack and showed the insect: it was a small praying mantis, green, and one of its long legs (B.J. said) was missing. B.J. reached for her drink, but in taking it she let the praying mantis slip to the veranda floor, near Heather. B.J. went for it, but when she came close Heather tipped her glass and let loose a stream of gin on the back of the thing, dousing it. The praying mantis twitched one of its legs, made a feeble half-spin with its body and then was still.

'Look what you did!'

'Shame,' said Miss Poole.

'They eat other insects,' said Miss Male, 'but I think you've killed it.'

'Sorry about that,' said Heather. 'I hate *dudus*.'

Miss Poole sipped at her drink and spat. 'What *is* this?'

'Why, it's cherry brandy,' said Heather. 'Isn't that what you said you wanted?'

'The poor thing's croaked,' said B.J. still looking at the dead insect. She plucked it by one leg and took it to the bed of African violets, where she scooped a tiny grave and dropped it in.

'You're a sentimental thing,' said Heather to B.J. 'It was just a *dudu*, after all.'

'They're quite beneficial,' said Miss Male. 'They eat other insects.'

'I think you did that on purpose,' said Miss Poole.

'I did,' said Heather. 'I hate *dudus*.'

At dinner, oil swam on the surface of the cold oxtail soup, the toast was burnt and looked like slices of coke, the butter was frozen solid, the meat bloody, sinewy goat, the potatoes crisply uncooked. Heather, who had clocked each bit with her egg-timer so that it was certain to be underdone, filled all the plates and took great delight in giving Miss Poole large inedible portions of the stuff.

B.J. mentioned the praying mantis again ('The poor thing didn't have a chance'), but none of the women responded or commented on the meal or called attention to the fact that the corpses of several flies were floating in the soup tureen. Heather had planned to fuss and blame the cook if the subject of the food was raised; no one mentioned it. The three guests ate slowly, with disgust and incredulity, and Heather even managed to force seconds on everyone by saying, 'I'll have to throw this away if you don't clean it right up. I hate to throw good food away, especially here where so many Africans go hungry.'

Plates were passed and filled.

An added, unplanned, but to Heather delicious discomfort occurred over coffee when, without warning and just after nightfall, the electricity failed.

'I think I should pop over to the school and see that the girls are all right,' said Miss Poole, rising.

'Surely,' said Heather to Miss Male, 'that Miss Verjee can deal with this. It's simply a power failure.'

'Miss Verjee gets all the donkey work,' said Miss Male.

'Yeah,' said B.J. 'Coolie labour.'

'Did you say *coolie*?' laughed Heather.

'I mean she's always left holding the bag,' said B.J., 'while we're eating and having a good time.'

Heather, who was lighting her cigarette, laughed loudly, then coughed and finally seemed to choke into her fingers.

'We all do our jobs,' said Miss Poole quickly. 'Each of us carries a fair share of the load. Miss Verjee does no more or less than any of us.'

Miss Poole looked from face to face, realized she was standing in the darkness, muttered, and seated herself again. Two flashlights were produced, switched on and placed upright on their ends. They lighted the cobwebbed ceiling of Heather's living-room but little else. The four women sat in shadowy cricket-haunted darkness, grumbled about the Electricity Board and felt for their coffee-cups.

'Do you know anything about this, Miss Lebow?' Miss Poole asked at one point. She gave B.J.'s name a French pronunciation, Lebeau, which B.J. liked.

'No, how should I know anything about the electricity situation?' B.J. giggled. She added, 'Gee whizz, Americans get blamed for everything around this place!'

'Please don't be offended,' said Miss Poole. 'I just thought you might know. You have dealings with them, haven't you?'

'We all do, don't we?' B.J. asked. She swivelled her head at Miss Poole, trying to make her out in the darkened room, and repeated, 'Don't we?'

'Well, I was thinking . . .' Miss Poole paused. 'Oh, never mind, Miss Lebow. I don't know *what* I was thinking.'

'How absolutely mysterious,' said Heather. She offered a second cup of coffee and, filling Miss Poole's cup, succeeded in pouring some squarely on to Miss Poole's foot.

One of the flashlights dimmed, grew orange and then

faded out completely; Miss Male managed to revive the
flagging conversation by commenting on the dead flashlight: she gave them all a little spiel on leakproof batteries
which, she claimed, were not leakproof at all. B.J. and
Heather both had flashlight-battery stories. Heather's was
pointless, but B.J.'s, which was about being in Piraeus late
at night with only a flashlight and using this to find her
way to the hotel, caused the others to murmur with interest.
B.J. said that she had always wanted to sell the story as
a true-life adventure to the Eveready company to use on
their ads, 'but they weren't Eveready batteries. I'm not
sure what kind they were, to tell the truth.' Inevitably,
the conversation turned to servants' foibles. Heather told
a story about her cook in Nairobi whom she had told that
she was going right next door for lunch; when she returned
she found him standing sullenly amid the brooms, the floor
polish and canned food, in the store-room. He had thought
she had told him to stand in the store for lunch. The others
offered stories: Miss Poole's was about Julius's inability
to distinguish *r* and *l*, B.J.'s was about her gardener's
amazing ability to tell the time of day to the minute by
aiming his forearm at the sun and gauging the angle of
his elbow. Heather sneaked gin into her coffee-cup and
became drunk. By the end of the evening she was puffing
her cigarette and blowing the smoke at Miss Poole in the
darkness.

The score was even, Heather felt.

The following week B.J. and Miss Male gave their dinner
party. Heather beamed when B.J. entered the room wearing a barkcloth sarong and carrying a large platter of grey
porridge and smaller dishes of pumpkin leaves and hard
red beans.

'We're going to eat African style,' B.J. announced,
passing the porridge. 'Something different for a change.'

African beer was brought, a thick, bitter liquid, lumpy with crushed kernels of corn and served warm in sticky gourds. B.J. sat on the floor, drank with relish and scooped up the beans with a ball of porridge which she held in her right hand. Miss Poole sipped at the beer, nibbled at the beans and fell silent.

'This was B.J.'s idea,' explained Miss Male.

'It's bloody marvellous,' said Heather, who was pleased to find the meal revolting. She glanced at Miss Poole, who was delicately holding the gourd of beer but no longer sipping. Her lips were pursed; her porridge was untouched.

'Mood music, anyone?' asked B.J. She put on an African record of drumming, chanting and rattling bells, a Congolese funeral ceremony she said she had picked up in the States.

'Did you say *funeral*?' asked Heather. 'They don't sound as if they're in mourning to *me*!'

'What do you expect?' asked B.J. 'They're Africans, aren't they? They have their own way of doing things.'

'Last week you were telling us that Africans are the same as everyone else. *You* said it, not me.'

'Well, they are,' said B.J. 'It's just that –'

'Why don't you join us?' asked Miss Male. B.J. was still squatting on the floor, bent over her bowls of food.

'It tastes better like this,' said B.J., smiling and tucking the top of her slipping sarong into her brassiere.

'In-credible,' said Heather softly; in a louder voice she inquired, 'Do I understand that all Africans up-country eat this? I mean, your common or garden nig.'

'They wouldn't eat anything else!' said B.J.

'It's lacking in certain essential vitamins,' Miss Male put in. 'Which accounts for the lethargy in Africans, sometimes mistaken for laziness –'

'You read that in an American book, am I right?'

'It happens to be a scientific –'

'Oh, I don't mean to be nasty, Pam,' said Heather. 'I just never agree with these simple theories. Africans *do* have such disgusting tastes. Ants, monkeys, fish-heads – have you ever heard anything so sick-making?'

'There's a lot of nutrition in fish-heads,' said Miss Male.

'You tell 'em, Pam!' said B.J. from the floor.

'It seems an uninspired fare. In Nairobi, of course, the diet is quite different, but then so are the people. I must say I'm not mad keen on this mush.'

Feeling personally challenged, Miss Poole ate her entire helping and drank her gourd of beer. When she tipped up the gourd she saw a small cockroach inside, clinging to the wet wall and flicking his antennae. She put the gourd down, said she felt unwell, and left.

'Do you think she's going to puke?' asked Heather after Miss Poole had gone.

'I hope it's not the food,' said B.J. 'I really tried hard –'

'Surely it's not the food. No,' said Heather, 'there's something wrong with that woman.'

A week later it was Miss Poole's turn to give the dinner. Heather wondered at first whether Miss Poole would dare; it would be asking for a rematch. The invitations were typed by Simon and sent out. On the appointed evening all the women were present and chatting cheerfully about the new school badge Miss Poole had designed, with its motto lettered in a flapping scroll at the top, *Daisies Are Our Silver*. Miss Poole served a stew made of vegetables and fish-heads. The fish-heads floated at the top, their scaly jaws agog, eye-sockets empty.

The dinners continued without let-up, B.J. and Miss Male's sometimes very pleasant, Heather's and Miss Poole's always made painful by cold-blooded bitchery and booby traps: ants in the sugar bowl, collapsing chairs ('Was that caused by white ants or bore beetles, do you suppose?' Heather had asked Miss Male while Miss Poole sprawled in tumbled disarray on the floor), knives and forks horny with old dried food, glasses with lip-rending chips in their rims. The invitations went out regularly every week; now the score was never settled.

What Heather considered her most successful move was the evening she paid her gardener and his brother to beat on the walls and roof while the women ate their dinner. One crawled on the roof and thumped with a hoe, loosening the soot and cobwebs from the ceiling, sending it into plates and on to heads. The other boy walked around the house poking the walls with a thick pole. Once he poked the wall behind a picture; the picture flew off its hook and smashed. The noises were as regular and persistent as a poltergeist's. Only B.J. mentioned the sounds; Heather ignored her. 'Possibly an earth tremor,' ventured Miss Male. But nothing more was said.

The uncanny thudding, the batterings from the blackness outside, shook Miss Poole terribly. Banging and knocking in the night had always given her bad dreams or kept her anxiously awake; now she felt that somehow Heather had discovered this, her most private and nagging fear. That evening she had to be taken home by Miss Male and B.J., one girl on each of Miss Poole's limp arms.

In her turn Miss Poole invited the three over. They had their usual pre-dinner sherry on the veranda and then entered the dining-room. There was something irregular about the table, B.J. thought; she studied the places and saw that it was set for five. When they sat and were served (it was 'toad in the hole', sausages in Yorkshire pudding, one of Julius's specialties) the extra chair, the silver, the plates were in order (next to Heather), but stayed empty.

The extra place at the table caused the women to bunch together, bumping elbows. B.J. found the collection of clean plates maddening.

'Are you expecting someone?' she said.

Miss Poole looked surprised. 'I beg your pardon?'

'I mean, there's a ...' B.J. had a mouthful of sausage and could not speak. She grinned sheepishly and jabbed her fork at the plate, the silver, the napkin, the empty chair.

'Oh, *that*,' said Miss Poole. 'Yes ... um ... he said he'd not be early, but he told me we shouldn't wait for him. He'll be along directly.'

'*He?* So it's a *man*, ha-ha!' B.J. had swallowed her sausage. She showed her perfect teeth. 'How *about* that!'

Miss Poole saw that she had the floor. She twiddled their curiosity. 'Yes ... he's ... well, one does even at this age have the occasional male friend,' Miss Poole lied. 'Of course, he doesn't get all the way up here very often. That frightful road. They should do something about that road. It's a positive disgrace.'

'Mmmm,' murmured B.J. impatiently. 'But the man?'

Heather forked food into her mouth and appeared not to be listening.

'The man?' Miss Poole's brow furrowed. 'What man?'

B.J. tossed her head at the empty place.

'Yes, I see. He's from ...' Now Miss Poole stopped speaking and plastered mashed potato on her fork, broke two peas over that and wiped it with gravy from her knife. She chewed the potato carefully, working her jaws in what appeared to be an exaggeration of eating, then said, 'What was I saying?'

'He's from –' Both B.J. and Miss Male spoke, their voices rising together earnestly.

'Well, he's from Nairobi of course. A teacher.' Miss

Poole looked at Heather and said lightly, 'In point of fact, your former ... um ... school, Miss Monkhouse.'

Heather pressed her lips together and turned pale. With her mouth shut her face seemed to shrink. She put her knife and fork down; she ate nothing more. For the rest of the evening she smoked nervously, said nothing, and glanced furtively at the front door. But the man from her school never showed up.

Both Miss Poole and Heather quickly realized that it was impossible for them to have a show-down without involving B.J. and Miss Male in it. This worried them somewhat, for they now made no secret of their tactics, and the tactics were growing cruder and more obvious. At times, B.J. and Miss Male suffered nearly as much discomfort as Miss Poole and Heather. B.J. once sat in one of Heather's prepared chairs; Miss Male got a roach in her bouillon at Miss Poole's. But nothing could be done about it; all four had to be present or there could be no assault. And, while still realizing the unpleasantness the squirming girls had to endure, Miss Poole and Heather were extremely upset one particular day when Miss Male had a jigger in her toe and could not come. The dinner party at Heather's that evening was angrily cancelled. Miss Male, like B.J., was needed as a witness.

In their own time, when they were alone in the house they shared, B.J. and Miss Male calmed themselves by inventing games of their own. Whist, bridge and other games gave way to the building of intricate structures – houses, bridges, castles – with the deck of cards. There were late-night quiz contests in which Miss Male learned that Helena was the capital of Montana, P.T. Barnum said 'There's a sucker born every minute', and George Herman 'Babe' Ruth (b. 1895–d. 1948) hit a record seven hundred and fourteen homers while he was in major league baseball; B.J. learned the names of the Home Counties, the two beasts on the British coat of arms and the breed of the Queen's dogs. With the help of one of Miss Male's dish-towels printed with a map of the London underground, B.J. also learned the names of all tube-stations on the Northern Line. Miss Male tried but failed to teach B.J. chess. B.J. said they could use the chessboard just the same and she proposed a version of bingo. She cut the chess-board into two sections, each one containing five squares across and five down.

The game was called Gecko and they played it with passion, all through the empty East African nights. The far wall of the living-room lacked a window, and this was perfect: large squares, five across and five down, were blocked out in pencil on the wall; two chairs and a table were set up in front of the squares. The lights were switched off and the room left in darkness for several minutes. When the lights were turned on, the wall was quickly scrutinized for geckoes, the small lizards that lived in the crannies of the house. The first girl to spot a gecko and correctly give its position placed a button on the corresponding square of her gecko board.

'Lights out,' B.J. would say.

They would sit in the darkness and then, 'That's enough! Lights on!'

When the lights came on (they took turns flicking the switch) they would crane their necks towards the wall and shout the position of the hapless gecko.

'G-Five!'

'No, it's on the line! G-Four!'

'It's moving!'

'G-Four. It's still G-Four!'

'I saw it first, B.J. Don't cheat.'

'Oh, fooey.'

Sometimes there were arguments, often there were no geckoes, and cockroaches had to be used – big dark ones from the open drain outside the kitchen door. According to the rules the game could be played at any time of the day. If Miss Male came to the house alone for morning coffee and happened to see a gecko hovering on one of the pencilled squares on the wall, she was at liberty to place a button on the appropriate square of her board. It was not uncommon for a game to last for days, and one game played during a dry spell lasted three weeks. B.J. said it was the greatest game ever invented; it was not, she said, just any old way of killing time, but a way of killing time that had East Africa written all over it. Sitting in their house for hours at a stretch, each girl with a drink in her hand, bowls of peanuts and potato chips near by, they watched for geckoes and talked about themselves, about interesting men they had known and about things they had always wanted to do if they had a pile of money all their own. B.J. listened horror-struck as Miss Male told her about the war years, the bombings and air raids in London; Miss Male listened in amusement as B.J. told her about Disneyland, the fake castles and pink elephants, Los Angeles, the time she saw Ava Gardner on Sunset Strip. Miss Male confessed that she had always wanted to visit the States; B.J. said that she would not mind staying a while in England, seeing the Queen and her corgis, walking on a foggy day in London town while candles burned in holly-hung windows and groups of cassocked choristers sang old English carols.

Late one night, tipsy on two lagers, Miss Male told B.J. that her name was really Malinowski. B.J., who had refrained from telling Miss Male what her real name was (telling Heather was one thing, but you never knew how your room-mate would react if you told her you were a Jew), said, 'Lebowitz here. *Shalom.*'

'*Shalom,*' said Miss Male. 'Isn't that a giggle?'

They swore that they would invite each other for a visit to their homes after they left Africa, just to see what their countries were really like. They avoided talking about Miss Poole or Heather and dreaded going to the weekly dinner parties. But the dinner parties, if nothing else, made B.J. and Miss Male grateful for each other's good humour; the more bitchy the parties were, the closer B.J. and Miss Male became.

In the way that a sportsman playing an unusually difficult game briefs the critics beforehand on his own skill and his opponent's crooked strategy, Miss Poole gave special teas and excluded Heather, Heather gave special lunches and excluded Miss Poole; and each took it as an opportunity to slander the other. The teas and lunches were failures partly because the girls were unco-operative, but mostly because the vulgar slanders were not being uttered according to the agreed rules, in the presence of the opponent. Miss Poole hinted at alcoholism, nicotine-poisoning and nymphomania in Heather; Heather, whose imagination and experience exceeded that of Miss Poole, suggested baldly that Miss Poole's appetites ranged from the bestial with her cats to the lesbian with Rose. To both hosts B.J. said, as she had once said to Heather, 'I don't repeat rumours, not even *to* people about the *same* people. I wouldn't tell you what I heard, because it's not fair to you ... I hate gossip, especially here, you know ...' Miss Male concurred with B.J., although she added that she might be tempted to phrase it differently. And they would both, B.J. and Miss Male, troop home across the grass, and calm themselves with a drink, a talk and a game of Gecko.

Miss Poole's teas continued, but in stony silence. And Heather developed a special way of inviting B.J. and Miss Male to her house. She would jump out from the hedge of bougainvillea as they walked back from their noon class, act surprised to see them and say, '*Lunch?*'

Urgency, need was in her voice, but not kindness. The first time she did it, B.J. shrieked she was so frightened. Heather persisted; she wanted their company as witnesses to her own suffering and to Miss Poole's perversity. At the same time she did not want to appear disappointed by the girls' refusal. She could only do this by pretending that the well-planned lunch invitation was extended on the spur of the moment, simply a bush courtesy. Slowly Heather learned a habit of abruptness which bordered on ritual, almost not an invitation, more the uttering of an aggressive formula. It seldom worked. Heather's lunch invitations were usually turned down.

There was no way Miss Poole or Heather could make the lunches and teas compulsory for the girls. They contented themselves with their attendance at the weekly dinner parties and it was plain that everyone was involved in the feud: the girls were witnesses, but close enough to the action to be harmed.

For a time, Miss Poole and Heather left slander and gossip and used new tactics. The thought of pestering Heather outside the dining-room came to Miss Poole by chance when, one day after asking Heather if her cook could help pick the coffee in the school garden (it was ripening fast; some of the berries had already dropped and rotted), Heather replied indignantly, '*Hapana*, no! Jacko is not going to help the girls with their chores. He's a cook, not a *fundi* on coffee. I won't allow it!'

'Everyone has to do his share. Julius was out there this morning –'

'If Julius wants to pick coffee that's his *shauri*,' said Heather. Whenever she talked about Africans she interlarded her speech with Swahili words. 'Jacko has *kazi mingi sana*, masses of work to do –' Heather continued to rant.

Miss Poole watched Heather reddening in anger, and she decided that there were simpler ways to get at her than giving a dinner party.

And at the same time, seeing how she had let herself be riled by Miss Poole, Heather made a similar deduction.

They were possessive about their servants. If there was any privacy at all in the school compound it was in the kitchen where the women and their servants carried on an exclusive exchange. Bush custom forbade anyone listening in on one of these conversations or interfering with the servants' duties. Practically everything in the compound was shared: dutch ovens, electric kettles, hair-dryers, typewriters, three-way plugs, phonographs, sewing materials and even, in times of real need, clothes. The servants were not common property; each was expected to be loyal, to maintain silence about what went on in his employer's house and to take orders from no one except the woman he worked for. Servants were seldom loaned. Although the women did not treat them particularly kindly (B.J. and Miss Male did not count; their gardener was a schoolboy, their cleaning woman was simply a part-time char), no one was allowed to talk to another's servant, much less give him an order.

It was with enormous anger therefore that a week after asking Heather if Jacko could help with the coffee-picking Miss Poole saw, from her office window, Julius staggering across the grass to the library, laden with a set of encyclopaedias, followed by Heather, whose hands held only a sprig of jacaranda. Miss Poole wanted to rush out of her office and scream at Heather (and tear the blossoms out of her hands: Miss Poole had planted that jacaranda herself and this was the first year it had given forth flowers). She had a more rational thought.

The next day, on her way to class, Heather saw Jacko high on a ladder against an unused building which Miss Poole intended for conversion into a library annexe and reading-room. Jacko was painting the wooden window frames green.

'Jacko, come down here this instant!' Heather cried in English. One of the schoolgirls was passing. Heather did not like to speak Swahili to her servants while the girls were around; if the girls showed no signs of going away Heather spoke Swahili in her coolest British accent. Jacko hesitated. 'Do you hear me? I said, come down straightaway!'

Heather made a sign with her finger. Jacko understood. He placed his large brush over the hanging bucket and climbed slowly down the ladder to where Heather stood.

'What the devil are you doing?' The schoolgirl had now passed. Heather repeated her demand in Swahili.

Jacko faced his curling toes. Spots of green paint glistened on his muscular forearms and torn shirt. 'The *memsab* say to me paint this house, Jacko.'

'Which *memsab*?'

'*Mzee*,' said Jacko, 'the old one. Missa Poor.'

'The bloody cheek,' muttered Heather. She thought a moment, then said, 'Well, you're not doing it right. You go ahead, but paint the windows. I see you haven't done the windows.'

'Windows, madam?' Jacko's eyes opened.

'The glass, everything! The windows, the walls, even the roof!' Now she spoke slowly in English, with gestures and a big smile, as if to an imbecile. 'Go up ladder quick-quick. Take brush and paint. This paint. Paint whole house nice. Then paint, paint, paint' (she swished her hand), 'paint, paint. Make house all green. Aaaaalllll greeeeeeeeen.'

'Aaaaalllllll greeeeeeeeen,' echoed Jacko. Now he had his real orders, from his own *memsab*; he ascended the ladder happily.

Miss Poole stopped him, but not before he had painted the entire end of the building: the window-glass dripped, the door was streaked, the gutters, the brick walls, the threshold – everything gleamed a bright green. Jacko had been furiously lashing paint on the roof tiles when he upset the bucket, his last can of paint. He went to Miss Poole to ask for more.

'Let's have a look,' Miss Poole had said.

'*No*,' she whimpered, shamelessly and piteously, when she saw the huge green end of the building. Her shoulders shook, her mouth compressed; she knotted her fingers and squeezed the blood out of them. She knew she could not punish Jacko; she stood helpless before the building, wondering how many gallons of turpentine it would take to scrub the paint from the porous brick. The paint dripped in steady plops from the green roof to the wide green leaves below, making the stalks nod a mocking yes yes yes.

'That will be all, Jacko. *Kazi kwisha*,' she said sadly, 'no more work.' She gave him a shilling, sent him home, and a short period of mercenary activity had begun.

When the wind was right, Julius burned rubbish near Heather's house. The stinking, choking fumes permeated Heather's clothes on the line, lingered in the kitchen, fouled her bedroom and made Jacko's eyes water.

Jacko pitched lighted matches at the cats and coaxed Sally into eating a dead mouse, green with mould.

Julius, tiny, adept at stealing, jacked up Heather's VW

and pilfered all four wheels, leaving the car aloft on wooden blocks. Heather fretted, accused, threatened to call the police; Julius replaced the wheels, but let out the air.

Jacko dropped a twist of his own excrement on the front steps of Miss Poole's house. Miss Poole stepped in it. Julius disgustedly cleaned it from her shoe with a stick. When he finished the chore he collected some bees in a paper bag and lobbed it through Heather's bedroom window. Heather was stung on the lip, Jacko on the neck.

Jacko stuck the swollen discoloured head of a colobus monkey on Miss Poole's front gatepost.

Julius slipped a bull's pizzle into Heather's meat-safe.

It had all started with a suggestion from Miss Poole: 'The wind is just right, and there is plenty of room to burn rubbish over there.' Then no suggestions were necessary. Jacko and Julius were of different tribes; in addition, their loyalties to their employers were strong, their identification with the separate households complete. They had been longing to get at each other and, with the consent of their *memsabs*, had their chance at last. It went on two weeks, from the burning of the rubbish to the secreting of the bull's pizzle; at the end of two weeks it verged on the tribal, a personal feuding which at first did not involve Miss Poole or Heather. The servants fought with each other, sabotaged each other's bicycle and cooking pot, and from the kitchen windows shouted insults: each accused the other's mother of having copulated with a hyena to produce him.

The women had complained vehemently. Miss Poole brought Sally to Heather's house and demanded to know why the cat was ill; there had been no reply from Heather but, happily for Miss Poole, Sally vomited the digested remnants of the mouse, and a few other meals, on to Heather's carpet. Heather had dragged Jacko to Miss Poole's and shown her the bee-bite on his neck (Heather claimed that she had not been bitten, but Rose had seen her applying alcohol to a bite and had reported this to Miss Poole). Then the attacks stopped, the servants were battling each other in private and the situation lurched into a new dimension. Heather and Miss Poole knew the games had changed when briefly, one afternoon, there was nearly violence. There had never been violence before. It was not supposed to be part of the game.

B.J. had seen it. She described it to Miss Male as 'crazy, weird, awful really'. In the field between Heather's and Miss Poole's, near a dusty fat-limbed frangipani, B.J. saw Julius squaring off with Jacko. Heather stood at some distance behind Jacko, Miss Poole and Rose behind Julius. B.J. heard Heather screech, 'Don't just *stand* there, Jacko. *Hit* him!' Jacko closed his eyes and slapped Julius across the face, his loosely made fist hitting sideways. When Jacko opened his eyes and saw what he had done, saw Julius gaping dumbfounded and pained at him, he turned and ran. Julius looked mournfully at Miss Poole, who said, '*Napenda?* Did you like that?' Julius shook his head no and then dashed after Jacko. B.J. started to hurry away. At the edge of her garden she looked back and saw the women still facing each other, shooting glares, motionless, their arms folded. Rose's body was inclined towards Heather, as if at any moment she would rush up to Heather and nip at her furiously like a maddened hound. The cooks had bounded through the hedge (broken twigs drooped) and were now out of sight.

They never came back. Their relatives carted away their bicycles and paraffin lamps. Without cooks, Miss Poole and Heather began buying expensive packaged soup, canned meat and (in a country which grew oranges, pineapples, avocados, paw-paws, guavas) fruit juice canned in Israel. Neither woman, in her whole time in East Africa, had ever squeezed an orange. They cursed the foolishness in their cooks that had made them desert. The women now knew they could expect no help from anyone, though each had privately nursed the unworded hope that her cook, venting tribal hatred, would permanently disable the other's cook, forcing her to buy canned fruit juice.

The showdown marked the end of the games, for it was violent and could have ended in actual harm to the women, a fist-fight, hairpulling or worse, as the cooks ran off leaving them to face each other. As it was, the women simply went back to their houses and sulked. The games had turned from a ritual of hateful play to hate itself; the symbolic gesture of dislike was now explicitly violent. The figged fist of the early harassment had become a fist.

No new cooks were taken on. Miss Poole and Heather stopped speaking. The weekly dinner parties, the teas and lunches ceased. B.J. and Miss Male had suffered through the meals and now they worried because there were none. Classes continued at the school as always, in ordered hours of mindless play, and at four o'clock, when the girls bounded on to the playing fields, each woman disappeared into her house, camouflaged in a clutter of dense African foliage and flowers. With this silence, the games froze into motionless hatred.

12

Silence

'She's a bitch, she hates me and she's dangerous. Apart from that I know sweet blow-all about the Memsab. Maybe she's out haunting a house.' Heather wrung a pencil as she spoke. She was in Miss Poole's office, sitting in Miss Poole's chair. B.J. stood at the doorway. She had asked where Miss Poole was.

'She might be sick,' B.J. said.

'Let's hope so.'

'That's not a very nice thing to say.'

'I think you'll find,' Heather said angrily, 'that *life* isn't very nice. For anyone. It's worse for women.' She changed her tone. 'Besides, you Americans say sick when you mean ill. When we say sick we mean puking. I didn't mean any harm to the old bitch – puking's not so bad, is it?'

'Who knows?' said B.J., hunching. 'Sometimes I wish I was born a man. They don't seem to have problems like ours, do they? I mean, you once said so yourself.'

Heather stared at B.J. 'That's an odd thing to say. You wish you had been born a man.' Heather continued to stare. After a pause she said softly, 'But if you *were* a man, I think I'd marry you.' Again she paused and turned her eyes to the window. 'I'd marry anyone.'

B.J. blushed. 'I think I'd better be going. Boy, I sure hope Miss Poole's okay.' She ducked out, wiggling her shoulders, pulling her sweatshirt down so that it fit snugly around her bottom.

Miss Poole was not well. She had told Rose, who conveyed the information to B.J. and Miss Male, that her chest hurt. She thought it was her heart. She claimed to have had two heart attacks since the day Jacko slapped Julius, three weeks previous, when the silence started. She had been absent from the school for both periods, each about a week long. During these absences she stayed in her house and sent Rose to the office with a note containing instructions for the teachers and saying in a P.S. that her chest pains had come back and only rest and tea would relieve them. On these days she could be seen through her front window, sitting in her chair, her elbows on her knees, hands clasped under her chin. When she appeared at the office she looked older, thinner, her skin deathly pale; and her dress stained and creased with sitting. This shabbiness and age was enhanced by a dryness in her face, as if she were dying not from a weak heart but by being slowly dried out.

During Miss Poole's absences, Heather acted as Head-mistress. She tried to change as much of the school routine as possible before Miss Poole doddered back. She shuffled schedules of duties, took the mothercraft and flower-arrangement, gave Miss Male drama and some English, ordered different sets of books, fitted new locks to the file cabinets and generally horned in on everything that concerned the administration of the school. She purged 'Daisies Are Our Silver' from the morning assembly and ordered the girls to sing (which they did in grating harmony) 'Land of Hope and Glory'. Heather lied that the 'Land' referred to in the song was East Africa; she knew, with a certainty that gave her joy, that Miss Poole sitting in her room across the empty compound could hear the girls singing. She was sure Miss Poole hated the song.

After the song, Heather used the little inspirational talk

to slander Miss Poole. Miss Poole had always taken as her subjects 'Our Friends the Earthworms' or 'Consider the Ant'. Heather spoke to the girls in a confidential, conspiratorial way.

'I must announce once again that Miss Poole says she is ill. Of course, there is very little we can do about this. We have prayed to God for her speedy recovery and, you see, nothing at all has happened. God will make her well when He sees fit, for He is all-knowing and knows all the nasty thoughts that a person thinks. He usually has good reasons for doing things, or not doing things, as you know. For my part, I am here and doing my level best, and I hope you appreciate how things have improved since I began acting as Headmistress . . .'

'Bosh,' Miss Male would whisper to B.J. in the back of the room.

'She's got her nerve,' B.J. would reply.

But Heather wanted to be friends. She used Miss Poole's absences to make friends with Miss Male and B.J. She told them about herself, what a madcap she was; she chirped that she was glad Miss Poole was ill because this might convince the Memsab that she should give up teaching; and then, in a fit of depression she would say that they all should pack up and go home. 'She's a bitch,' Heather said one day; she added, 'I'm a bitch, too. We're all bitches, aren't we?' 'On the other hand,' Heather said later the same day, 'she might still be playing games with us.' Excessive clowning was also part of her gesture of friendship to B.J. and Miss Male; unfunny and often painful, it embarrassed them both. One day she carried a tall moulting sunflower into the Staff Room. Holding it with her elbow up, she hummed and pretended to waltz with it.

'What's that?' asked B.J., looking up from a pile of exercise books she was marking.

'It's my new lover. Isn't he *gorgeous*!' Heather laughed and went on humming.

Heather's hair, usually blonde-streaked, had started to go white. Miss Male said this was simple neglect: Heather had stopped colouring it. B.J. insisted that it was a case of nerves. Her hair was turning white with madness. Miss Male said pooh. B.J. was so angry at Miss Male's contradiction that she guiltily broke her non-gossiping vow and repeated, to prove her point, a conversation she had had with Heather the day Heather wore a cardboard ape-mask to a staff meeting Miss Male had not attended. Miss Poole had just returned to work after one of her heart seizures and called the meeting to reverse all the decisions Heather had made in her absence. Heather had cut out the mask from the back of a cornflakes box and wore it throughout the meeting, in protest. It grinned while Miss Poole spoke of treachery, appealing to B.J. and Miss Verjee to stand by her.

After the meeting B.J. had said, 'That mask just kills me, Heather. You're a riot!'

'That's only the outside you see. You can't see the awful heartache I have in here,' said Heather solemnly through the grinning mouth.

'I hate to say this, but I think Heather's going nutty,' said B.J. to Miss Male. And there was no way of helping her because the two older women refused to speak to each other: the games were over, there was silence.

This truculent silence was much more worrying for B.J. than any of the games had been. The dead flies in the soup, the chair collapsing, the bad food, the cooks' desertion – these appeared silly, girlish, now hardly hurtful. B.J. said the silence was 'crummy for the school and the craziest thing I've ever seen'. Miss Male said that something had to be done to prevent the women from killing each other.

The dead silence made contact impossible. In the stillness, even with the sun shining on the flowers every day, both girls sensed violence hiding.

The stillness threatened violence, but what made this even more upsetting for B.J. was that she had discovered contentment. What she thought intolerable was that people could hate each other in a silly, pointless place where peace was possible. She had successfully passed through her weeks of confusion and anger at the same time as Heather and Miss Poole had their games, before the silence. B.J. knew she had achieved a personal peace when, late one night, she said to herself desperately, *What the heck am I doing here?* She sipped at her warm beer and replied calmly, *I am sitting on the Equator with my Gecko board, watching two geckoes creeping across the squares on the wall.* B.J. was fine and, because of this, she was all the more worried about Heather. She felt something terrible was going to happen.

B.J. had suffered through the games; so had Miss Male. B.J. had suffered embarrassed anger, Miss Male abdominal pains. Miss Male's ills could be traced directly to the bad food and the discomfort of her weekly dinners. B.J.'s anger was more complicated, and she was glad it had ended. While she was angry she had thought of quitting Africa and going straight back to San Diego.

It had started with the first dinner at Miss Poole's when Miss Male had carved the joint and Heather had argued and shouted, and when Julius had dropped the chocolate *mousse.* She had noticed it at the time, but the evening had altered her. She had passed through six weeks of denial.

She was at the Horse and Hunter with Wangi. The owner, a seedy alcoholic named Fitch, was behind the bar. B.J. bought Fitch a drink and he returned the favour by chatting to B.J. He said that he had seen her in there before;

he asked her name. B.J. told him, adding that it was 'sort of German'.

'But you're a Yank –'

'Not really,' said B.J. and as she said it she realized that the denial was starting in earnest. She had never lied before in her life. But once she had said that she was not really an American, Fitch's curiosity was aroused.

'You *sound* like a Yank, if you don't mind my saying so. A certain bloody clankety-clank, if you know what I mean.'

'Well, I *studied* there. I suppose I picked up the lingo,' B.J. said. 'The *lingua franca*, ha-ha.'

'So you went to school in the States?' Fitch showed no signs of giving up.

'Oh, a year here, a year there.'

'What about San Jose?' Fitch stared at B.J.'s sweatshirt. He pronounced the *J*.

'That? Yeah, I was there a little while,' B.J. lied. She fidgeted. Fitch looked suspicious. B.J. explained by fabricating a tale about having studied abroad. In her confusion, Wittenberg was the only European university she could think of. Hamlet had gone there. 'It was very nice at Wittenberg. Very neat and clean. You know the Germans.'

B.J. pleaded with herself, *Why am I lying like this?*

'So you're not a Yank,' Fitch said.

'My mother is. My father – he's –'

'Yes?' Fitch was interested.

'He's actually a Russian *émigré*. Really. Named Lebowitz. He had to leave Russia when the revolution came.'

'He must be a pretty old geezer.'

'*Nein*. Not very,' said B.J., 'not terribly.'

'The revolution was in 1917, am I right? Let's suppose your father was twenty when –'

'He's not young,' said B.J., groaning inwardly. Lying about dates was impossible; one date was always connected to another. They had to fit. *What's wrong with me? Why am I saying this? Daddy's not from Russia – he's from Pine Bluffs! Oh shoot.*

'Anyway,' said Fitch, 'I hate the Jerries worse than the Yanks. Too bad you're half-kraut –'

'Well, what difference do nationalities make? We're all the same, aren't we?'

'No bloody fear,' said Fitch. 'I fought Jerries for years. Hate 'em.' He got himself a drink. 'Half-Yank, half-kraut,' he said, eyeing B.J. 'Blimey, you Yanks are a fooking mixed lot. Now me, I'm English right through. Bugger the lot of them.' He drank.

'I'm an African,' said Wangi. He had trouble following the conversation. He said nothing else.

'I guess I'm a little bit of everything,' said B.J. and thinking, *And I'm a little liar, too.*

Afterward, B.J. examined her lies. They saddened her. The only explanation she could think of for her strange behaviour was that she was tired of being an American. She was sick of English people pointing out niggling differences between England and America. She had always looked for similarities and expected everyone else to do the same. Now she was denying everything; she blamed Heather for it mostly, all of Heather's remarks which began, 'You Americans ...' She had once understood Heather and all other English people. She had pitied them. Now she could not recapture the understanding; she felt oppressed. She was certain of this when she heard herself say to Heather one day, 'I forget if I'm supposed to be teaching third period. I've not seen the shed-jewel.'

'You're doing the geography then,' said Heather with her finger on the teaching schedule.

B.J. thanked her and, as she walked away, thought, *I've not seen the shed-jewel. My God!*

On other occasions she actually heard herself say petrol, possport, the gulls are doncing, biscuits and tea, the boot and bonnet of the VW, a spanner in the works, tomahtoes, the hot-water tap, I tore my knickers, jolly good, sticky wicket and a dozen others. It wasn't American. B.J. wasn't even sure if it was English. She hated herself even more than when she had, to her horror, heard herself say *running wadder* and *on doody*.

Largely she hated herself because she had discovered why she was doing it. Over five months of bitchery, inquiries, nasty comments, explanations, arrogance, without an American in sight had upset her. It had changed her and she wondered how she could ever change back. She was a chameleon, out on a limb, and had chosen a difficult camouflage. It had been just talk, idle chatter, but the effect was definite: 'I've not seen the shed-jewel.' And that, she decided, was what Africa was for everyone: a lot of talk. Nothing more. It was darned unfair.

She had been cheated. She remembered her first thoughts of Africa, standing in the oval-domed lobby of the airport in New York with thirty other Peace Corps Volunteers (serious little buggers with sunglasses and handbooks and rucksacks, greeting each other in too-loud Swahili). She was about to board the plane for East Africa, but she took no notice of the others. Images of Africa had come to her in a rushing flood: drums, dancing, gaiety, Humphrey Bogart bars, fly-blown, the ceiling fans slowly revolving, the sweating settler faces, one man in an immaculate white suit playing with his gin and tonic; the lush forests overgrown with vines that obscured the forest paths; women naked from the waist up, their firm black melon breasts gleaming in the flakes of sun that filtered through the leafy trees; the shriek and tattoo of fantastic-tailed birds in the dense jungle where no white foot had trod; the blazing heat and mosquitoes and she, B.J. Lebow, lying in her tiny cot in a mud hut under the ripped mosquito netting, trembling with malarial chills, her faithful servant making tea on the Primus and saying, 'You nice *mzungu* help us and teach white man's tongue'; intrigue, mystery, the uncanny tales of the native, ghouls limping out of graveyards, heads shrunken and dangling from the straw eaves of huts; the peevish British boozehound in his up-country post, drinking the days away and plotting to strike a blow for merry old England, his thin angular wife gagging on her sixtieth cigarette of the day, the dry hacking cough of the woman ('Let's get out of this godforsaken place.' Cough, cough. 'I don't know why you stay here year after year, you bloody Welsh bastard ... If only we were back in Clapham now ...') and the benign but murderous planter ('Come back here, you black devil, and fetch me a drink ...'), long afternoons on the veranda looking at the ploughed fields, the sun setting on the Empire, the strong noble faces of the Africans bent over their work, naked children gambolling in the sparkling creek; and, oh Heavens, yes, the drought, the disease, the attacks on the manor farm, the throats of mission docs cut and the blood running on to their oriental carpet, the one they haggled for in Port Sudan on their last home leave; the all-night throbbing of the jungle drums. And where were they, Mistah Kurz, Allnutt and Rose, Cecil Rhodes, Stewart Granger, Burton and Speke, Stanley and Livingstone, the Sultan of Zanzibar, Karen Blixen on a lion-hunt, torchlit and horrifying, anthropologists living for years in a village studying the movements of tribes and raising their nut-brown children on mangoes and Spengler, the oily Portugee plying his trade in used tommy-guns up and down the Zambesi and drinking sparkling wines in quaint Mozambican cafés, Arabs with long knives hidden under their cloaks who'll slash you for a piastre and pry the gold out of your teeth, the white hunters with sombreros and leopard-skin sweat-bands, Papa Hemingway bushwhacking through lion-country and swigging out of flasks ('There's a damned fine set of horns on that gazelle ...'), and the delicious *veldt* stretching for miles under the eye, the lovely road that runs from Xtopo into the hills, the snows of Kilimanjaro, *The African Queen, The Heart of Darkness*, Nairobi, the hordes of pygmies and their pygmy king crowding up against your ankles, the revolutions, revolutionaries, counter-insurgents, freedom fighters drawing a bead on a caravan of Landrovers ... *Safari* ... *simba* ... *Watusi* ... *bundolo* ... *voodoo* ... *ungawa* ... *ungawa* ...

It was not Africa. It was a lot of baloney. It existed only in movies, books and people's crazy imaginations. B.J. looked hard for it all, for just a teeny trace of it, and when she was sure none of it existed she made plans to go home. It was, after all, the best place to go: Hollywood was a shortish drive up the freeway and that is where most of Africa was. She had to go home, for not only did none of the romance exist, but also nothing of Africa held fascination. Africa ('savage, wild, dark, spectacular, mysterious') was the dullest place B.J. had ever been, the biggest zero on the globe (and B.J. had drawn some pretty big blanks: everybody in Spain lisped, Greece was queersville, and a dark little man in San Juan, offering her a bunch of flowers he held waist high, had displayed his poorly concealed and tumescently rosy member in the bouquet – '*El sabor lo dice todo*,' he had urged). The Africans were the limit, the most predictable, reactionary, sentimental drunks she had ever met. The famous big game – elephant herds, rhinos, prides of lions, all the beasts that the travel agencies bragged about, were in game parks or zoos, a great disappointment mainly because it was no different from Southern Cal. Who wanted to go to the Snake Park in Nairobi and pay two shillings just to see a python? B.J. had expected the exotic, the mysterious at least. It was not asking much – mystery was easy. But Africa was not mysterious, only disorganized, slow and dull. If there was a secret, it was that there was really none. And the sun in Africa, the blazing heat? It had been hotter in San Diego.

She had brought with her a little notebook, an old-fashioned one with a shiny black cover, unlined white paper sewn to the binding, and a red cloth spine. She had planned to write impressions of Africa, sights and scenes that moved her, fragments of conversations, maybe even a few poems. The notebook was, five months after her arrival in East Africa, empty; the blank white pages were going limp and mossy in the humidity. On page one there was a date; beside that, the beginning of an entry: *Africa is ...* The entry was unfinished, and there was nothing else in the notebook except her name and on the cover, framed in a little label, the title, *African Impressions*.

Africa so far was only the endless staring of Wangi, the bitchery of Heather and Miss Poole and the noisy aimlessness of the girls at play. And what really galled B.J. was the fact that the dull bitchy things were happening there, in East Africa. It would not have been so bad in San Diego or L.A. where those things were supposed to happen. But East Africa! And this pettiness made the place even more ordinary, no different from the plainest sleepiest hick town in the Mid-West. The pettiness would have robbed Africa of exoticism, if indeed Africa had ever been exotic. It would have been mean to write all that down in *African Impressions*. The whole hick aspect and the nasty women would pass into nothingness as they had passed into silence. There would be no violence. Violence needed motives;

there were none in Africa. Several times, B.J. tried to write in her book, tried to finish her little entry, to give a definition to the place. It was no use. Africa was dull, boring and sometimes people in Africa were pointlessly cruel. When this all became apparent, she had no desire to write it down or even tell her father in a letter; she just wanted to go home.

And then it came to her: *I'm going home eventually. It doesn't matter. I only have another year here and then I cop out!*

Shortly after, she asked herself the question, *What the heck am I doing here?* and gave her calm reply, *I am sitting on the Equator with my Gecko board,* and so forth. She knew she was at peace. There was no point in dropping everything and quitting. She would never be able to explain to the Peace Corps how she had been cheated. The fantasies that had flooded her in the New York airport, all those Hollywood images of Africa, now deeply embarrassed her. On the plus side, Miss Male was nice, the weather wasn't bad, the job was simple; she might even, she thought, be doing her own thing, making a little contribution that would give the East African gross national product a boost. It would not be hard to stay, only a pain in the neck.

Something she found hard to believe, and had never thought would happen, was that she occasionally forgot where she was. It happened a number of times, too often for B.J. to write it off as simple absentmindedness. She might be just opening her eyes in the morning or engrossed in one of the high-minded magazines the Peace Corps mailed her constantly or making herself a jelly sandwich. For those minutes, sometimes as many as five, she could have been on a little family vacation, with her father and mother out of earshot, reading the *Los Angeles Times* on the grass.

Eventually she remembered where she was, but it was

not the drumming or the wildebeest or the lions (where the heck *were* they anyway?) that suggested the reality of her distance. It was, in fact, her Zenith Transoceanic radio that made her know that she was not in San Diego. After the snack or magazine she would flick it on and get horrible static: wheeling shrieks, morse code, wobbling unfathomable music or gibberish from somewhere in the Indian Ocean. When a station did come in, it was an awful reminder of how far out you could be: Big Ben booming an intro to a B.B.C. quiz, a crackling news broadcast from All-India Radio, vowelly Portuguese from God-knows-where, nasal French from Rwanda or the Congo, the platitudes of the gospel radio station in Ethiopia, an unmistakably Negro voice talking about the rising standard of living on the Voice of America, the familiar harridan screeching the thoughts of Mao on Radio Peking, or a loudmouth on what B.J. privately thought of as the Foice of Chermany. All the broadcasts said they were being beamed to Africa and the Far East, and it was painfully obvious to her that she was not in the Far East. All the broadcasts talked about Africa's achievements in development schemes, some even (ha-ha!) spoke of Africa's dark mystery. B.J. listened once to the B.B.C.'s 'Book at Bedtime' which, that evening, was a story about Africa by Joe Conrad, read in a Peter Lorre voice. During the entire broadcast B.J. was in stitches.

It was the radio that shocked B.J. into reality, but the reality was a dull outpost that she knew she would be leaving soon. The year would go quickly. When she shut off the radio and sat in silence, as she did after twenty minutes of searching the short-wave band for Frank Sinatra, she knew where she was. The silence was heavy. But there were worse things than silence.

What if, she thought, there *were* murderous Arabs and yelling, spear-throwing Ubangis? What then? It might have been much worse than the silence. It might have been dangerous instead of dull. *If I can stand the silence I've got it licked.* And remembering that she was going home, that indeed unlike Miss Poole and maybe Heather she *had* a home to go to, was enough reassurance to wipe out the weeks of lying and denial, and the embarrassment at having been cheated in a big way. She dropped her English accent and Russian-German heritage and stopped saying 'shed-jewel'. She was an American. The more she thought of this the prouder she became. She loved America. She would never have a bad word for it again. America was a comfortable place crammed with invention and ease. The silence in Africa simply did not matter. She had made a big mistake, the biggest lulu of her life. She would correct it when she went home. Calmness came to her at the same time that agony came to Miss Poole and Heather; it was a certain satisfaction, deeply pleasing, in having realized how wrong she had been about Africa and how she was now right. Her good humour returned and she made jokes about Africa, not nasty ones, but ones that showed that she did not belong. And one day she said to Miss Male, 'Really, Pam, you should visit the States. It's the greatest place on earth. We've invented so many things. You know, *we* invented Africa.'

Wangi remained, B.J.'s only contact with the real Africa. She continued to date him – that also in silence, since he seldom had anything to say. She dated him more out of a sense of obligation to the Peace Corps than out of any affection for the man himself. She often thought of breaking it off, not seeing him any more, but she knew that this would be a mistake. For one thing, Wangi was what the Peace Corps laughingly called a 'host country national' and had to be known and understood. To stop seeing Wangi would mean a complete withdrawal from Africa, a withdrawal that would make her no better than Miss Poole or Heather or any of the other unpleasant white people who lived in East Africa and who never had anything to do with Africans. And she knew it was possible that without male company she would develop the same symptoms of bitchiness that Heather had. A husband or a male friend would cure Heather; she had almost said as much when she said, 'I'd marry anyone'. So seeing Wangi every week was necessary, first, because he was an African and B.J. was a Peace Corps Volunteer in Africa; and second, because he was a man. Women needed men, if only to get out of the company of other women.

Wangi was not dangerous. He was Africa, with all of Africa's dullness, simplicity and emptiness, with all of Africa's pretensions to order, the tribesman with puffy ornamental scars hidden (she was almost sure) by his dark suit and neat shirt. B.J. had at first pitied him, listened to his stories of terrorism with nervous impatience. He would mumble and brag and, as he went on, grow drunk. His speech became thick, barely coherent as he swigged gin. In the middle of a slow sentence he would slump in his chair and go to sleep. B.J. would rouse him with a poking finger in his cheek and help him out the door, say good night and *kwaheri*. For a few moments she would hear him stumbling in the dark outside, groping his way to the road. The next week he would return and apologize. He was harmless.

But the stumbling in the dark worked on B.J. She often thought of it: the black man muttering, stumbling through the flowerbeds at midnight, not even bothering to ask for a light – then silence, he was away. She thought of this pathetic image and wanted to help him. She wrote to her former teachers at San Jose and asked if there were any scholarships available for an African student. The teachers wrote promptly; they also wanted to help; they replied in long sympathetic letters asking about Wangi's qualifications. There might be something for him, they said.

Excited at the prospect of getting Wangi into a university, B.J. quickly wrote a letter on Wangi's behalf. He was, she wrote, from the poorest country on earth; he had not even owned a pair of shoes until he was twenty years old and he had had a hard life in the village. But he had good potential: he was very (B.J. searched for an honest word) *curious*, she finally wrote. Before she sent the letter, she talked to Wangi, whose eyes filled with tears when B.J. told him of her plan.

'You just have to qualify and you're in,' she said.

Wangi gazed, no longer tearful. 'But you said the scholarship was for an African.'

'Sure,' B.J. said. 'But if you want to go to college you have to qualify. You know, take tests, finish school, study, ha-ha.' Wangi's habit of giggling was infectious; now whenever she talked to him she laughed, she did not know why.

Wangi's face clouded over. He lowered his eyes. 'Write those people a letter. Tell them my cousin Wilbur is the District Education Officer. They'll take me.'

An emptiness grew in B.J.: there were airy sighs where hope had been. Wangi had done nothing in his life. He had been nowhere. The only book he could remember having read was *Coral Island*, abridged for overseas students with a vocabulary of a thousand words; he had forgotten the author's name. The application form to San Jose State would be entirely empty, a silence on the page representing the silence in the country: darkness, people stumbling drunkenly through the flowerbeds and muttering softly – not even the noise of curses breaking the silence. B.J. had not really thought much about him until the teachers in San Jose asked. She did not send her letter. She told Wangi he would have to wait a year. She did not have the heart to tell him that in a year she would be in the Golden West.

13
Orders

There were fleas in Sally's fur, small winged specks which could have been mistaken for dark grains of dirt. After Miss Poole had stared at them for several minutes she saw that the specks were moving; they were alive and crawling from hair to hair.

She could not kill them, although she had that afternoon bought a can of flea-powder from the Indian *duka* down the road.

'The best thing known for *dudus*. Wery scientific,' the Indian had said, overcharging her.

Miss Poole had watched him wipe his mouth on his shirt-front and began to have doubts. She looked at the Indian and saw a killer.

'Tell me, isn't it true that Hindus don't kill flies? I thought they didn't kill anything, in point of fact.'

'Jain. You know Jain? They are even not killing small *dudu*. They are letting mice wander quite free in their compounds,' said the Indian. 'They are being wery foolish, not modern. It is modern to rid food and body of all crawling insects and *dudus*. Isn't it?'

Miss Poole took the flea-powder but doubts nagged at her. The Indian was too eager to kill. By the time she reached her house she had almost given up the idea of dusting the fleas.

She continued to stare at the fleas, cradling Sally in her left arm and holding the can of flea-powder in her right hand like an oversize salt-shaker (it had a circle of holes punched in the top). The words of the Indian came back to her, and she began to hate him, nearly as much as she hated Heather. With these feelings of hatred awake in her she thought, *There is too much killing and cruelty in the world*, and hated Heather all the more. The worst thing about killing was not the savagery it betrayed, but the effect the killing had: death upset the order of things when the death was unexpected. Cruelty made men stupid. These were Africa's misfortunes: sudden death and cruelty produced by intruders. First the migrations, the hordes of little black people trekking like a column of ants down from Ethiopia, across from West Africa, what the map-makers called Negroland, converging in the Congo basin and around the Great Lakes to squabble over territories they claimed for themselves. Similar in temperament were the Arabs, the Portuguese, the Indians; Miss Poole saw it as a great wog onslaught, killing, plundering a jungle and a jumble of ant-people that had never known order. It was a deathly bloody process that only the people like her father had attempted to reverse. These far-sighted people, the only men she could respect, had imposed a humane order on East Africa. For a brief period there were farms and, on those farms, people and animals; the people and animals lived in harmonious candour, not very different from Miss Poole herself, in her house in the highlands, with Sally on her lap and the fleas in Sally's fur. There was stability and she saw it all in a little parable on her lap. As soon as one of those living things was killed, the order was disturbed, death had begun and the jungle moved closer, a fat vine-tendril snaked into the schoolhouse window. Miss Poole put the flea-powder down and stroked Sally.

There were still intruders, as selfish as Arabs, and as

sensual. But no one saw that while some people in Africa were intruders, others belonged and did no harm; these last considered East Africa their home. They behaved as Christians. God's little fleas did not intrude; they were part of the order, gentle, small, harmless, and at the mercy of the loud and the large, the corrupt, the blasphemers.

Heather was a killer, her intrusion could only mean murder. Miss Poole was sure of this. But she had no idea of what Heather's precise plans were. Until Heather arrived everything had gone smoothly at the school. Miss Poole was proud of the record: only three pregnancies, good discipline, a well-trained hockey team, no student strikes or complaints about the food, a successful parents' day and tree-planting. The school, except for the inevitable white ants and bore-beetles, was in good repair; the coffee yield had been high. And the teachers seemed to get along well.

With Heather it had all changed. Miss Poole saw her as a demon-figure, corrupt, lustful, lower-class with a put-on accent and falsely trilled r's. Her arrival had coincided with the onset of Miss Poole's debilitating illnesses. This made sense, for at one level corruption was physical and germ-ridden. Miss Poole went over her illnesses as if touching cautiously at scabbed wounds. Since Heather's arrival her heart trouble had worsened, the dull ache had become a sharp stabbing pain in her breast; she could feel a wad of blood constricted in an artery, leaking like an old faucet, each drop causing pain as it hit into the dry hollows of her heart. A large soft carbuncle had formed behind her ear, the size of a florin; Rose had lanced it with a heated needle: black goo had shot out and hit the wall. There was an almost weekly bout of malaria: chills, flushes, a searing headache that went on for days, scarcely relieved by quinine; her fevers had never been so bad. Waking with a start one night Miss Poole had felt for the lamp-cord and grasped a long furry caterpillar which bit her, it seemed, with the length of its body: red pustules were raised on her palm; these took a week to heal and the whole thing looked like an ogre's bite, each fang-mark gone septic. She had had prickly heat, rashes, heat-stroke and muscle fatigue made worse by chronic insomnia. At every turn she encountered fierce pain or discomfort. Roaches scrabbled from between bread-slices on the table. A bat dropped from a roof-eave into her window box and turned green; other dead bats turned up in cupboards, linen closets and market baskets. Julius was far away and could not help. Only Rose was left to witness the ordered bewitchment of all the creatures that had lived so peacefully before. The germs had obviously multiplied, the little beasts had run amuck; even the cats were contaminated. Sally had scratched Miss Poole on the neck; the wound had festered.

It was a restlessness which Miss Poole saw as devilish, inspired by Heather. Heather had brought the disorder, cruelty and death which Miss Poole associated with all the intruders that had ever plagued Africa. Because of Miss Poole's cursed illnesses and absences, the school had run down: indiscipline was common, bills were unpaid, a roof beam in the science laboratory was chewed to bits by white ants (again a diabolical order from Heather carried out; the ants had nested in, but never chewed through a beam before). The beam collapsed, sending thick roof-tiles into a cupboard of glassware, smashing everything. The coffee bushes were coated with fungus, the corn stalks with fuzzy brown smut. And all this in the short time Heather had been at the school, most of it during the silence that followed the painful dinner parties. Miss Poole had thought Heather an intruder from the first, but she did not grasp the full malevolence of the woman from Nairobi until she read an article called 'The Power of Love'. She had found the article in a *Reader's Digest* that had been donated with some used books to the school. It was an old issue, Miss Poole thought, but the message was timeless. The article spoke of a certain vicar from a village in Somerset who could make plants blossom and grow through the power of his love. Conversely, by not loving (hate was beyond him) he could make a plant wither; exercising this loveless-ness, he could make a dog grow wild and bite his master, he could make petals drop or sturdy animals keel over. It seemed unearthly, but there were witnesses to the vicar's powers. And Miss Poole was convinced that, better than the vicar, she knew how vile emanations could work on lovely things, on simple folk.

In the single school term, now almost over, that Heather had been at the school, Miss Poole had watched the merci-less sabotage of all her hard-won order. In addition to the unpaid bills, the smashed glassware and the infected crops, the girls had grown wild. They adopted Heather's high silly voice and idiotically italicized speech; they dressed like slatterns; they yoo-hooed, gobbled and used skin-lightener and blotch cream; they spent hours pulling their kinky hair into nests glistening with greasy bubbles of vaseline. The rock gardens and terraces were in a shambles. The domestic staff was threatening a strike. And one night, without a word of warning, the building that Miss Poole intended for conversion to a library and reading-room, the one Jacko had painted green, burned to the ground. The day before the fire the workmen had succeeded in removing all Jacko's green paint. Miss Poole knew it was an act of Heather's godless will and she fearfully concluded that Heather was a witch. Heather would have to go.

Miss Poole covered her face with her hands; she moaned into her palms. She felt her viscera freeze, and shud-dered. She saw Heather's design: Heather wanted to be

Headmistress – it was simple, so bluntly cruel, Miss Poole had not thought of it before this moment. Why else had Heather willed Miss Poole's illnesses and then taken over the school, occupied it like an invading Arab? If the stories told about her were correct (and they probably were: there was always a grain of truth in the East African gossip), then this was not the first time Heather had resorted to a fiendish means to get what she wanted. The stories from Nairobi were inconceivably grotesque. Miss Poole tried to stem her moaning by biting her hand. It was no good; when she bit, the moans came louder. Sally yowled and hopped to the floor where she stood with her back arched, her fur spiky with terror.

It was night, noisy with the swamp-dwellers tuning up. Miss Poole sat in the darkness of her living-room, the cats slumbering on chairs and draped in sleep on the floor. Rose squatted near the window. When Miss Poole spoke, Rose crept closer.

'You like me, don't you?' Miss Poole spoke in her heavily accented Swahili.

'Yes, very much,' said Rose in a low voice. Her head was reverently bent down.

'Am I a good woman?'

'You are good.'

'When I am here you are happy?'

Rose emitted a long *aahhhhhh*. She pressed her dry hands together and rubbed them. In the dark it sounded like leaves rustling, a strange sound since in that lush place the leaves seldom rustled.

'Am I good to you?'

'You are good. You give us food to eat.'

'And clothes.'

'Such beautiful clothes,' murmured Rose, feeling the hem of her long soiled dress.

'The flowers in my garden, my food, my house, everything I have belongs to you. It is all yours.'

'You are my mother,' said Rose. 'You took me into your house and cared for me when everyone called me bad names and said they wanted to kill me.'

'You are safe here.'

'Yes.'

'Rose,' Miss Poole said, 'have you ever felt a white person's hand?'

Rose uttered the verb in amazement. When she said it again, Miss Poole remembered that the only word she knew for feel was the same as for smell and taste.

'Have you ever held a white person's hand with your hand?' said Miss Poole. She had not realized how difficult this was to say in Swahili.

'Not in my life,' said Rose softly.

'Here. Take my hand,' said Miss Poole, lifting her hand from the arm of the chair and holding it out. 'Here.'

'I can't see.'

'Come here.'

Rose crawled slowly towards Miss Poole. She woke two cats that were snoozing on the floor; they pattered into the corner, hushing with surprise.

'Closer.'

Rose did not take the extended hand at once. She felt for it; when her fingers struck it she drew back. Shyly she teased the darkness again with her fingers and touched the hand, tapped the soft flesh with her forefinger, felt the slack skin, the thin birdbones of the fingers. She could have been caressing a sleeping chick. She worked her fingers around it and then clasped it with two hands, frantically; she sobbed, a phlegmy choking deep in her throat that shook her hands and the hand they held.

'You mustn't be afraid,' said Miss Poole. 'I'm not afraid. I know you love me.'

'Yes, I love you.'

'Can you feel my hand?'

Rose continued to sob. 'It is beautiful. So soft.'

'Hold it tightly,' said Miss Poole, her voice growing hard. 'And listen to me. Are you listening?'

Rose whimpered yes. She nodded: Miss Poole saw the flash of her dark glasses, the shadow of her queer beret bobbing up and down.

'Someone here wants to kill me,' Miss Poole said coldly, giving the word kill, *kufisha*, a snarling sibilance.

Rose shrieked. She let go of Miss Poole's hand and rolled on the floor, her shriek dying to a slow agonized wail. There was a crash in the darkness, a cat upsetting a vase; the bump of padded cats' paws on the floor.

'Rose! Stop it! Listen, Rose!'

Rose put her face against the carpet and continued wailing through clenched teeth, now softly, prostrate before Miss Poole in her armchair.

'We must be very, very quiet or someone will hear us. I will repeat: someone wants to kill me. This person wants to live in this house and be Headmistress. If that happens you know what will become of you.'

'We will die,' Rose moaned.

Miss Poole was pleased with the reply. Rose saw that if the order was disturbed, death would be the result; the fallen tree, cut by the intruder's axe, crushed the life out of small ground-dwelling creatures. Rose understood. It was the kind of logic only the innocent could comprehend: they knew of the kind balance, the calm order, that love caused. And Africa was the last stronghold of this order;

everywhere else death and iron, people crouched in cold sewers, the air poisoned by filthy machines. Africa breathed peace, not a skull-shape on the map, but the head of God, Christ brooding over the rest of the threatening world.

'You don't want to die, do you?'

'No, madam.'

'I can help you, can't I?'

'Yes, madam. Only you.'

'Will you help me?'

'Yes, anything. Who wants to do this bad thing?'

'I don't know –'

Rose sighed.

'– but I know how we can find out.'

'Tell me.'

'The secret is in the new *memsab*'s house –'

'Madam Hethala,' said Rose, giving the name a Swahili shape.

'Yes. That one. You must go to her house when there is no one around. Make sure her dog is away – perhaps you can lock it in one of the sheds. Don't be in a hurry. Go next week, when we are busy with exams. Look in the drawers, on the tables, everywhere, and bring me letters, chits, notebooks, anything with writing on it. Tell me everything you see in that house. Be quick and don't let anyone see you. If someone sees you, leave immediately. I think there is something in that woman's house that will tell me who the murderer is. When we know, we will be safe.' Miss Poole took a deep breath. The strain of saying all this in Swahili was too much for her; she had searched for words that would not craze the girl – the excitement might drive Rose mad, and Miss Poole did not want that. She wanted help. In English she added, 'Whatever you find will be valuable. I am sure she is hiding something from us.'

Miss Poole was weary. She yawned and felt a tug at her ankle. Rose was on the floor, with her hands curled around Miss Poole's foot, like a village girl paying homage to an elder. Rose held on tightly, her arms gleaming white.

14
A Banana Peel

B.J. decided to give Wangi until the end of the term.
After that, she could drop him and make friends with the
clerk at the school, the vegetable-sellers, possibly even
the Indians down at the shops. Face-to-face, the Peace
Corps called it; getting to know the Host Country
Nationals. She would be seeing the Peace Corps rep in
Nairobi after the term ended; he would be sure to ask how
she had been spending her time. B.J. had a lot to tell him
and was glad the end of the term was only a little over two
weeks away.

But there was still what B.J. called 'the village bit' that
remained undone. When she knew that she could do
nothing for Wangi's further education, since his only
qualification for being a foreign student was the fact that
he was foreign (and you couldn't get much more foreign
than plain ignorant), she agreed to go with Wangi to visit
his village. Wangi borrowed his cousin's car and picked her
up early on a Sunday morning at the school.

It started raining as soon as they left the main road,
and the rain seemed to come down harder and harder as
they travelled farther into the bush on the rutted back road.
The car swerved; Wangi fought to keep it on the firm
grassy hump in the centre. On both sides of the road, creeks
had formed; the bare gleaming tyre-tracks had reddened
in the rain in a way which, contrasted with the freshly
doused green of the plants at the side, made the road

seem almost diabolical, winding like the road to Oz where
Judy Garland met those crazy animals. The sky was so grey
and low that B.J. felt she could reach out of the window
and snatch a handful of it.

There were few trees that B.J. could see, for the view
on both sides was blocked by tall elephant-grass. Heavy
now with rain, the grass curled towards the road and made
a long fringed awning which brushed both sides of the car.
Wangi drove in silence.

They had been on the road for half an hour when, without warning, the vast peeling face of a bus, its eyes
orange, appeared from out of the awning of grass twenty
feet ahead, in the centre of the road. Wangi slammed on
the brakes; the car skidded; Wangi spun the steering wheel
as if it was the handlebar of a careening bicycle. The car
became light and rose to let the bus roar past, flopped with
a crunch and came to rest, still on its four wheels, in the
grass at the left side of the road.

B.J. screamed and held the dashboard. At once the windows steamed grey, opaque.

Wangi slapped the steering wheel, making it vibrate.
'Sheet,' he said, 'look at us!' He grinned.

'Let's go,' said B.J. 'We can't stay here.' She felt pain
but could not identify it as injury or tell where it was. She
wanted to get out of the car to see if she had been
hurt.

'Yes,' said Wangi. 'When it stops raining. Then we go.'
Wangi sat back and smiled at the steering wheel.

'How far is it to your village?'

'Maybe more than a mile, maybe two.'

'We can walk,' said B.J. decisively, yanking the door-
handle. The door did not open. She pushed the door with
her shoulder, while jerking the handle. 'I don't get it. How
the heck –'

Wangi put his hand on B.J.'s wrist and lifted her whole arm away from the door-handle. He slid beside her and then put his other arm around her neck.

B.J. froze. It was the first time Wangi had ever touched her. She didn't like it. Her senses were jarred by the surprise of the oncoming bus, the shock of the car leaving the road, the clouded windows. She wanted to get out of the car and flex her arms, search for bruises. Her wrist was being squeezed; her neck hurt from the pressure of Wangi's arm which was forcing her head forward.

'Come on!' she said. But Wangi did not let go. The rain pattered on the roof of the car, gently, innocently; and all around the car, showing in droplets on the steamed windows, were the dripping tapes of glass, most of them squashed and bent from the car's impact.

'I said, *come on*!' B.J. muttered through tensed lips.

Wangi seemed to grip harder; but she was not sure. And then she heard herself saying '*Come on, come on*,' and realized what it meant to Wangi, for as she said it he was coming on, holding her more tightly, hugging her in a half-nelson.

'*Cut that out!*'

Wangi released his grip and drew back slowly towards the steering wheel, his eye widening, his hands slipping to his knees.

'Thank you,' B.J. said firmly, fixing her hair, squirming slightly. She did not look at Wangi. Once again, she tried the door, this time with determination, shoving it with her shoulder. The door creaked and slumped open against the grass. B.J. wriggled out, stepped in mud and then pushed the door back into place. With her hands in front of her face, she parted the grass; it scratched her as it brushed her arms and legs, but still she struggled through its abrasive wetness like a breast-stroking swimmer, until she splashed into the road. She stood in soggy sneakers, soaked and aching. She began to cry, an infant's blubbering, her face wet with rain and tears. Her hair had gone ropy; she tasted bitter strands of it in her mouth.

Ten feet down the road the grass swayed, then parted like a curtain. Wangi broke through, agitatedly wiping his face with his handkerchief.

When B.J. looked at him she stopped crying. His wet suit was wrinkled and shapeless; there were green seeds stuck to his collar and hair; his cuffs were spattered, his shoes large with gooey mud. He looked pathetic, like an orphan turfed out into a rainstorm in his Sunday best. B.J. felt curiously guilty and ashamed; she was certain she had said the wrong thing. *Come on*, she had said; only an American could be expected to understand that, and only an American would. Wangi had touched her (her neck and wrist still ached), but had made no suggestion. It was she who had unthinkingly urged him. He had said nothing; he had remained silent the whole time, as he was now silent, eyeing her from his distance down the rainy road. In the silence was all of Africa's cruel ambiguity, what people took for mystery; it was not mystery, B.J. reminded herself, simply an overpowering silence in which nothing really moved, no one stirred, where there could be no bad intentions because there were no intentions period. It was a huge bluff, as in a poker game where the man keeping the inscrutable poker-face held blank cards: they were not winning cards, but empty, frayed bits of cardboard. If there had been malice (but of course there hadn't), it was the pathetic malice of the inept pretender. She stared at Wangi wiping his face and hands with the shrivelled handkerchief (he did it fecklessly; it was still raining), picking the green seeds from his collar, and the panic that she had felt left her completely. Her head cleared. She could not remember anything that happened in the car.

'We can walk,' she said calmly.

Wangi was surprised, but he took the hand she offered him and in the rain, their feet sucking in the mud, they squelched up the road.

After the first mile the rain stopped. B.J. was soaked; when the sun came out her drying clothes chilled and chafed her. The little cuts from the grass on her legs and arms rose into red welts. Her wet sneakers were heavy with mud. She felt miserable and longed for a dry spot, anywhere to sit down. She wanted to bathe, be alone, rest between clean dry sheets, eat something ... A pain shot through her belly.

'I'm hungry,' she said to Wangi.

Wangi sighed. 'I'm sorry,' he said after a while; he looked down in mournful terror.

B.J. screwed up her face. 'Sorry? For what?'

'You're hangry.'

'Not *angry*, silly, *hungry*. *Hun*. *Hun*-gry.'

Wangi smiled, looked around and, seeing what he wanted, dashed into the grass, punching the broad blades away from his face. He returned after several minutes, his arms full of bright green balls. He said they were oranges.

'*Green* oranges?'

Wangi nodded.

'But oranges are supposed to be *orange*. That's why they're called oranges,' said B.J.

'Is it?'

'Yes. I mean, these things probably aren't ripe. They're the wrong colour.'

'No, this is the only colour. They're always green, even when they're ripe.'

'That's why they call them oranges, right?' B.J. smiled.

'You call them oranges, we call them *machungwa*.'

'Okay, hand one over. I'm game.'

B.J. regretted the green orange almost as soon as she started peeling it. The rind got wedged under her fingernails; the bitter juice stung her open cuts and soured her mouth and squirted into her eyes. She sucked; the juice dribbled down her arm and into a sore near her elbow she had not noticed before. Her hands became sticky and that discomfort, with the dampness and wet clothes, the chafing and searing pain of fruit juice on her cuts, made her all the more anxious to go back to the school. She had never in her life felt so miserable. She spat pips with a disgusted *pah*; half of them landed, in a long amoeba of yellow saliva, on her sweatshirt.

Wangi stopped sucking his orange. 'There,' he said. He sprayed a juicy mouthful of seeds in the direction of some small grass-roofed huts just off the road. To B.J. they looked like haystacks, and badly piled haystacks at that. About twenty feet away, a gaggle of small naked children dawdling in a mud puddle looked up and stared in disbelief at Wangi and B.J. The children cautiously approached and then followed behind, trooping like filthy elves. They held bunches of mud-spattered grass which they shook ceremoniously and, because they saw a white person, chanted '*Mzungu, mzungu, mzungu*' in squeaking voices.

The whole village seemed to sag from the strength of the rain that had just passed. Flameless fires billowed smoke into the clearing while women languidly fanned the smoke with squares of tin. A mangy narrow-jawed hound with fly-specked sores showing over a basket of skinny ribs limped from behind a hut and began barking at B.J. Then the women fanning the smoke looked up and saw Wangi and B.J. The women were dwarfish, with gremlin wrinkles around their faces, their ear-lobes stretched into jiggling loops; they wore long muddy skirts. They shrieked in a chorus of short high caws and shuffled towards the visitors, a flock of flightless birds. One came forward and took B.J.'s hand. The rest gathered around, shyly picking at B.J.'s seed-stained sweatshirt, feeling the thick softness of her damp hair and all the while making their insistent crowing.

The old woman holding B.J.'s hand greeted her in Swahili.

'Missouri,' said B.J. It was her new Swahili, a practised American-type; the name of the Show-Me state was close to the Swahili word for good, *mzuri*. And 'Missouri sinner' was like the Swahili, 'Very good'. The joke was her own, private and satisfying.

The women were pleased that B.J. was well; they clapped their tiny hands and grinned broken teeth at her. One gestured for her to come and sit down in front of a hut. A rickety wooden chair was brought. B.J. sat gingerly. It groaned but miraculously did not break.

There was another groan, not from the chair this time, but from inside the hut. The women babbled and stepped back from the hut. The groaning turned to wheezing which grew louder: an old man hobbled through the hut door on a stick. He was tiny, bent and wrinkled like the women, with tightly kinked grey hair cropped close. He stood before B.J. and stared; his whole body seemed to breathe woodsmoke at her.

'My father,' said Wangi. The women murmured their approval and, some distance away, the small naked boys hooted and wagged their grass whisks.

'Tell him I'm very pleased to meet him,' said B.J., fighting off an urge to scratch a nagging itch that ran like a coarse zipper from her head to her feet.

Wangi translated. The old man said, '*Habari gani?*'

'Missouri,' said B.J.

The women yelped and tossed their heads, making their loose ear-lobes dance. The skinny dog pawed his way past the gleeful women; he startled B.J. by nipping hungrily at her hand. B.J. pulled her hand away and the dog leaped at her, but was caught in the ribs, mid-flight, by the toe of Wangi's shoe. The dog howled, flopped at B.J.'s feet and then trotted clumsily away.

'What's his name?' B.J. asked. The dog had frightened her. She tried to regain her composure. 'The dog,' she asked again. 'What's his name?'

Wangi said something quickly to his father in a vernacular that was not Swahili. The old man croaked a reply to Wangi which was greeted with laughter from the women.

'He said it's a dog,' Wangi explained. 'And he asks that don't you have dogs in England?'

'Tell him I'm an American.'

Wangi spoke again to his father.

This time the old man faced B.J. He grunted something, a heavy guttural which he repeated again and again.

'He's saying Coca-Cola.'

B.J. then listened closely to the old man again and realized that he was saying, 'Drink Coca-Cola'.

'He likes to talk English,' said Wangi.

'He does?'

The old man grinned.

'Coca-Cola Missouri,' said B.J.

The old man understood. He looked pleased.

'Where did you get your stick?'

Wangi muttered, pointing to the stick. Again there was laughter when the old man replied.

'He says from a tree.'

Gobbling, the old man thrust it at B.J. It was shiny from being handled; on the top end there was a knob, the rough carving of a monkey's head; at the other end, emerging from the gnarled shaft, was a battered simian paw.

'He wants you to have it.'

'Oh, no,' said B.J. 'That's *his*. I couldn't take his walking stick.' She shook her head at the old man and said very clearly, '*No*.'

The stick was withdrawn; the old man mumbled and looked sad. The women fell silent.

'What's wrong? Did I do something wrong?'

'You refused his gift. He says it is not good enough for a *mzungu* and that he is poor. You're supposed to take it if he offers. That's African hospitality.'

B.J. smiled at the old man and took the stick. The women clapped. The old man nodded and spoke to Wangi.

'He says you're his daughter now and you have to eat with him.'

'Why not?'

Food was brought, greasy stew and thick mush, which B.J., Wangi and the old man ate while the women and naked children watched. To the delight of the women, B.J. ate with her right hand and smiled after each mouthful. She wolfed the food down only because she was hungry – the food was awful; her own African meal had tasted much better.

'They think it is funny. They never saw a woman eating with a man before.'

'Where do *they* eat, for goodness sake?'

'Not with the men.'

When B.J. finished she felt as if her belly was full of rags; she felt dirty, sloppy, sick to her stomach. She wanted to lie down in a warm white room and be scrubbed with a large soapy loofah.

'What do they do here all day?' she asked Wangi wearily.

'Nothing.'

'Nothing at all?'

'They drink and waste their time,' said Wangi. 'Nothing happens here. Sometimes there isn't any food and they have to send a lorry with mealies from Nairobi. It's all rubbish. That's why we hate the British.'

B.J. had stopped listening to Wangi and was now listening to her rumbling stomach.

The old man muttered.

'He's telling a proverb,' said Wangi.

'Oh, I *like* proverbs. What does he say?'

'It's hard to translate. Lazy man tree, busy chicken. That's what he says.'

'Yes, but what does it . . .'

'It means, I think, it's better to be like a chicken that always pecks the ground than like the lazy person who is like –'

'A tree?'

'No. Like a giraffe, because giraffes look like trees.'

'But there aren't any giraffes around here.'

'There used to be. The British killed them all, like they killed us.'

'Tell him I like his proverb.'

Wangi turned to the old man, but saw that he had dragged himself to the side of the hut where he swayed, stickless, pissing.

'How will we get back to the school?'

'We can stay here. There is a bus tomorrow morning.'

B.J. panicked. 'I can't. I have a class.'

'It doesn't matter.' Wangi shrugged.

'Miss Poole will call the police if I don't show up. She'll think something's happened to me – I'll be in trouble. So will you, Wangi.'

146

'That car is stuck. How can I –'

'There are lots of people around here not doing anything. They'll help you pull it out of the mud,' B.J. pleaded. She changed her tone. 'I'm telling you, Wangi. I'm not staying in this place. I'll *walk* back to the school if I have to, I really will.'

Wangi rose slowly and called to some boys who were idling around a hut at the far side of the clearing. 'You stay here,' he said to B.J. 'We'll get the car out and I'll come and pick you.' He explained this to his father, who had returned to his low stool; the old man nodded and went on staring at B.J.

The women had squatted in a circle around B.J.; the old man faced her. She saw none of them. On the ground, embedded in the mud near her chair, she saw a small broken spear with a rusty blade. Where were the drums, the dancers with the lion-mane head-dresses, the fantastic-tailed birds? She had not really expected to find them near the school, but here she was in an authentic village and there was no sign of them. Perhaps they had been there before and this is what it had all come to: a small spear-blade rusting in a tropical slum. Near the hut there were sodden cigarette wrappers, a Coke bottle, crumpled boxes of tea, dog-turds. And all through the smoky compound, dirt and silence. One by one the women left, until there was only B.J. and the old man, soot blowing into their faces, flies gathering on their hands and arms and on the remains of the food in the cracked enamel bowls. Where the women had been squatting there was a pile of garbage: orange rinds, the frothy-sinewed spittings of chewed sugar-cane, limp banana peels. In this ripe pile of garbage was the image. Not drums, dancers or exotic birds, but a special laughable silence. Completing her unfinished journal-entry B.J. mumbled to herself, 'Africa is a banana peel.'

Her laughter startled the old man.

At dusk, the headlights of the car veered into the compound. B.J. walked stiffly to it. She was chilled to the bone. Her back hurt from sitting on the slumping chair; her legs ached from the chafing bermuda shorts; her skin felt patched and stitched with stinging scratches. She knew her hair was a sight: it felt thick and greasy. Her hands were dirty, for even though it was dark and she could not see it, she could feel the filth clinging to her hands like gloves. She yanked the door open. Before she got in she turned away from the headlights to the old man's little haystack hut and said softly, '*Kwaheri*, good-bye.' She thought she heard a small troll's voice, as if speaking from under a large stone, returning her farewell. She knew she was imagining it, for she paused and listened. There was silence in the sodden village. If there had been a sound, it must have been the wind in the broken grass.

She felt dirty, but free. Now she knew how explorers must have felt, coming upon muddy ruins deep in Africa after a year's trek. Filthy and tired and standing in silence, they looked beyond the ruins and the clutter of rusting spears to dense grass; they were hermits in the desert searching for the evidence of faith. Like hermits they were assailed by images which mocked and tempted: savage warriors, slim black girls, the lustful rumble of drums, fearsome yelling and, all around them, wet dripping trees and lovely birds. In these imagined scenes the explorers found release in faith, and a literature was born. It was understandable; they could not have reported the silence or the decaying deserted order. And they could not be blamed for their imaginings – sailors had once thought the piggish dugong to be a shapely swimming woman.

And B.J. selected her own image, more honest than the explorers', more comic than anyone had ever associated with Africa. A cartoon sketched itself on her mind: there were two characters, a fat white huntress in a pith helmet and a feeble, chuckle-headed pygmy wearing only a bone in his nose. In a bubble near the lady's head was: 'I'm head over heels with Africa – wait till I tell the folks back home!' The pygmy was munching a banana. The banana peel was under the lady's raised boot; she was about to step on it . . .

'Why are you laughing?' asked Wangi.

'I was thinking I haven't washed my hands all day. This is the first time in my life that's happened.'

'We can stop at my house.'

'Oh, no you don't!' laughed B.J. and thinking, *You pygmy*. 'Take me straight home, and drive slow or you'll kill us both. I've got papers to mark.'

A banana peel, a banana peel. The words tumbled in B.J.'s head. She felt happy. She would bring one back in a box and present it to the San Diego Museum of Natural History and say, 'Here, get a good taxidermist and stuff it!' She would tell Heather; that would cheer up the old sourpuss. Heather. B.J. had not thought about her or Miss Poole or the school all day; now she imagined Heather in the cartoon saying, 'I'm head over heels with this place.' *Poor Heather*, thought B.J. *She's just lonely*.

When they arrived at the school, B.J. turned in the seat and said, 'You want to go out again, don't you?'

'Yes, I do want,' said Wangi.

'Missouri. Well, if you promise to behave yourself, I will. But only on one condition. You have to get a date for my friend Heather Monkhouse. She's very sad these days. She doesn't see many men.'

'Yes,' said Wangi.

B.J. got out of the car. 'One other thing. Heather's very hard to please, so get your cousin, the Education

Officer. Then she *can't* refuse. She'll like him, won't she?'

'She'll like Wilbur. He's an important man,' said Wangi with respect. 'We'll go on Friday to the Horse and Hunter.'

'Sounds real good,' said B.J. and, twirling her new walking stick like a majorette, crossed the grass to her house.

'My God!' exclaimed Miss Male when B.J. entered. 'If you weren't smiling I'd say you've just been rogered in a swamp. Where in heaven's name have you *been*?'

'I've *been*,' said B.J. imitating Miss Male's English vowel, 'to Africa. That's where I've *been*.'

'You're keen on it of course,' laughed Miss Male.

'Of course,' said B.J. 'I'm mad about it.' She looked at her hands with disgust; shaking her head sadly from side to side, she said, 'Pam, really it was horrible.' She tried to say more, but she could not find words to describe the ugliness; it was a vocabulary she seldom used.

In bed, the peace she had felt before came again. This time it did not come from a recognition of what Africa was; it came from perceiving America; she dreamed of her father, a tub full of bubble bath, the San Diego Central Sophomore Hop, gleaming cars on the Freeway, the twenty-foot plastic doughnut in Pasadena, Frank Sinatra, pizza, I.B.M. machines and (laughing softly in her sleep), See ya later, alligator.

15
The Horse and Hunter

Sometimes people drove all the way from Nairobi simply to look at the signboard of the Horse and Hunter. It was a large creaking board, the sort found in front of an English country pub, symmetrically scalloped on its edges, worm-eaten, and hinged to a rusting iron bracket over the door. On it, a man togged out in hunting garb – peaked velvet helmet, scarlet riding coat, jodhpurs, high boots – crouched on a galloping horse. A curved hunting horn was strapped to the narrow saddle.

Before East Africa's independence, a white face showed under the hunter's helmet; the horse was a gleaming black. Two years after independence the local party officials gave the owner of the pub, Fitch, a choice: change the sign or close the place and leave the country. The sign, they said, was an offence to all Africans, a vestige of colonialism; it showed that Fitch hated black people. Muttering 'bloody minstrel show', Fitch re-painted the sign: the hunter's face was painted black and given thick red lips. The horse was painted white.

It was a much-publicized incident. The Nairobi papers featured stories on the re-painting and, under the headline *End of an Era*, printed pictures of Fitch glowering under the freshly touched-up sign. The Horse and Hunter achieved notoriety: a small dining-room and several guest-rooms were added to it; it was now an inn, Fitch an inn-keeper. Fitch became very popular with Africans. For the first time in twenty years, business was good. The Horse and Hunter now made money for the same reason it had lost money before. What was formerly dirt was now character. People drove up from Nairobi to have a look at the sign and see Fitch.

Fitch was filthy; he had always been filthy. Pig-faced, his lower lip protuberant under a stained moustache, stubby-armed and with fat hands, he was the sort of man who would have looked dirty even if he had washed. He had meant to marry; it was almost as if he had forgotten to, for he liked women. In his shack at the rear of the bar he kept a purplish-back Nilotic woman who, after the custom of her tribe, had all her lower teeth knocked out. He called her 'Auntie'. One month in 1956 all Fitch's hair fell out. It fell out in dandruff-spotted swatches; Auntie bought some gluey hair-grower from a village *mganga* which she smeared on Fitch's pate. This did no good: in a week the few remaining hairs fell out. Fitch was left with a smooth knob, crusted with dirt and ridged with crescent-shaped scars. The rest of Fitch's body was hairy: the hair curled like sour weeds on his chest and back and, on the nape of his neck, spiralled above his collar in a pelt. The thick tangles of fur on his forearms held flakes of dirt and grains of grubby shapeless matter that appeared to be decaying, like apple-cores in deep grass. He scratched himself continually, four broken fingernails raking across his soiled paunch; the scratching was a kind of strumming, as if his belly were a banjo.

He was a drunkard living unwashed in the East African bush, perspiring heavily, cursing in forces' slang ('the bugger shits through his teeth after two beers', 'I have to go drain my snake', etc.); he was known to the whites who visited the pub or stayed in the little hotel-annexe as 'a real Graham Greene character'. In fact, Fitch had read and enjoyed Graham Greene, and there was a time when he had consciously modelled his drinking and generally squalid appearance on the unhappy expatriates in the Greene books. He had always wanted to be 'a real character' and had worked at it, studied it at first, thinking that it would be good for business if he were grumpy, kept flea-bitten dogs in the garden and an African mistress in the bedroom, did not wash and refused service to what he called 'the fooking Yanks'. After several years of working at it, the character *was* Fitch; it was no longer a pose. He had become an authentic cranky drunkard, mean with money, evil-smelling, spitting tobacco into his moustache, scratching holes in his under-shirt, punching up Auntie, cursing Africa and hating England. Many people said they wanted to write books about him.

It was Friday night. There were no guests in the hotel; the last customer, a beard-pinching Sikh from the garage in town, had just left the bar. Fitch was angry. He had, against his will, struck up a conversation with the Sikh in the hope that the Sikh would buy him a drink. The Sikh talked about shock-absorbers, praised the British and exhaled his rancid betel-breath on Fitch who stood close, scratching his belly in four-four time and praying for the Sikh to say, 'Hev a vishkey, Feech'. After four whiskies the Sikh had wiped droplets from his beard, crawled off the barstool and stumbled into his car. Before driving away he relieved himself in one of Fitch's flowerbeds, in the darkness, a loud spattering on the leaves. Fitch kicked the wastebasket across the bar and considered flinging the Sikh's lip-printed glass into the road when he remembered that it cost two shillings. He tossed the glass into the steaming sink and decided to buy himself a whisky.

He had uncorked the green bottle when a distant engine, like a fat horsefly, hummed in his ears. It sounded like a car. If it was, it would stop. There was nowhere else a car could be going at night: the Horse and Hunter was on the Great North Road; beyond it were rocky hills, scrubland stubbled with dusty broken bushes and cacti, then Ethiopia, which Fitch called Abyssinia. He slid the cork back, replaced the bottle on the narrow shelf and walked to the veranda, two of his dogs nipping at him, the third howling at the far side of the garden. Above him the signboard creaked. He stilled it with his hand and listened. Yes, it was a car.

As soon as the four people entered the bar, Fitch knew he would get a drink. Two African men and two white girls. The Africans would buy him a drink, to prove to the girls that they didn't hate whites. One of the white girls he recognized as having bought him a drink before. So there were three drinks for sure, possibly more.

'Evening, Chief, what's your pleasure?' said Fitch to the large bald African. Fitch spoke in a hearty, maty way. Because he hated Africans he always took special pains to ingratiate himself to them; he knew that if he did not do this his contempt would show. And this African, Wilbur, was a senior civil servant and had become, in the few months he had been in the district, a regular customer at the Horse and Hunter. Fitch had no choice but to be maty with him and, in fact, could only really afford to be grumpy with whites. He forced a laugh and set up four glasses.

'I say,' murmured Wilbur pompously, 'I do believe I'm going to have a whisky and soda. Black and White brand, if you please.' Wilbur looked at Heather and B.J. and winked. 'I'm all for integration!'

'Well, fancy that,' said Heather under her breath. Only B.J. heard.

'Ha-ha, very good,' said Fitch gamely. He had heard the

joke a hundred times, had claimed to have brought it himself from Nairobi.

'What about the ladies, Wangi? Don't be a savage. Ask them.'

Wangi scrambled to his feet. He started to speak but was interrupted by B.J. saying, 'Beer for me.'

'Pink gin,' muttered Heather.

'I'll have a whisky,' said Wangi. 'Black and White, ha-ha.'

'Right you are,' said Fitch, fishing a beer bottle out of a tub of stagnant water.

'What are you having?' asked Wilbur.

'Me, sir? Oh, very kind of you, sir,' said Fitch gratefully, and hating the ungenerous Sikh even more. 'Whisky for me as well.'

Fitch passed the pink gin and the beer to Wilbur, who handed them to B.J. and Heather. Then he made the whiskies. 'Fook everybody in the bleeding world,' he toasted, with the drink already to his moustache. He lapped thirstily.

'Cheers,' said Wangi.

'Bottoms up,' said B.J.

Wilbur swirled his glass and watched the fizzing bubbles. 'Was that Schweppes soda you put in here?' he asked. 'You know I don't take anything else.'

'Schweppes it was,' said Fitch.

'Very good then.' He raised his glass. '*To the ancestors!*' he bellowed, and he poured the entire drink down his throat. When he had carefully unfolded his handkerchief, wiped his mouth and then replaced the handkerchief in his pocket so that three white points showed, he looked at B.J. and Heather. 'You're going to think I'm a rotter, but I don't know your names. Mine is Wilbur.'

'This is ...' Wangi began.

'B.J. Lebow. Pleased to meet you.'

'We've met before, I believe.' Wilbur said this in sincerity to most white women.

'Yes,' said B.J. 'Well, I was at your house, I mean. The party you gave when you were transferred here. That's where I met Wangi.'

'I'll tell you something,' said Wilbur genially. 'Wangi works for the Electricity Board. Don't let him shock you!'

Wilbur doubled up with laughter. B.J. smiled. Wangi tittered uneasily. Fitch didn't laugh; he decided to be sullen unless he was bought another drink. Heather remained conspicuously silent.

'You think that's funny?' said Wilbur to Heather.

'Yes,' said Heather flatly. Her expression of unamused impatience was unchanged.

'Then why aren't you laughing?'

'I don't feel like it.'

Heather was there much against her will, though when B.J. had first asked her to come along for a drink she had gladly agreed.

'With pleasure, dearie. Where did you *find* him?'

'Right here,' B.J. had said. 'I mean, he's Wangi's cousin.'

'*Wangi?* That *local*?'

'Sure, he fixed it up.'

'He did, did he? Well you can tell him to bloody well *un*fix it. Count me out.' Heather barked a laugh. 'I've never heard of such a thing. Oh, you *are* fantastic.'

B.J. pouted, 'Come on, Heather. Be a sport.'

'I *am* a sport. Ask anyone. But I'm not desperate. I hope I'm not offending you, but I don't like Africans.'

'But this is an African country,' B.J. protested.

'Why? Because you see a lot of black faces around? Don't you believe it, ducky. *We* run this country; *we're* in charge, *we* pay the bills. If we pulled out there wouldn't be a virgin or a shilling left in East Africa.'

'*We?* You mean us teachers?'

'No,' said Heather, pulling the hem of her dress down to cover her fleshy knees, 'the Western Powers.'

B.J. stared at Heather's badly made-up face: the mascara was thick, the powder had missed a few sunburned patches on her jaw, the lipstick made a false bow-shape on her thin lips. Heather's hair, the streaks that had been dyed, had gone greenish in the humidity. The loose flesh on her arms jigged as she swished her glass to and fro to mix the bitters. B.J. was speechless.

'They told me this would happen,' Heather mumbled. 'The people in Nairobi told me there was a lot of this going on.'

'Come on,' B.J. said, now uncertainly. 'You'll have a good time.'

'No, I won't. If you want to take your chances, you can. I'm not a trade unionist and I don't like blacks. I'm not going to risk my life for a free drink. I don't trust these blacks one single bit. The term's over next week. I can wait – then I'm going to Mombasa and really have a dirty old time for myself.'

'I'll bet he's nice.'

'Who's nice?'

'Wangi's cousin.'

'You mean you don't even *know* him? What next!' Heather laughed. 'If you Yanks want to play with the blacks, go right ahead. You're welcome to them. But not me, Bettyjean.'

'Gee, he'll be disappointed.'

'That's hard cheese.' Heather drank to demonstrate the finality of her words. She smacked her lips. 'I'm not going out with a black and that's final.'

'He's not any old African, you know. He's the District Education Officer. *I* thought you'd be glad.'

Heather's smile slipped from her face. Her lips were wet with gin. 'The *District Education Officer*?'

B.J. nodded.

'Did you tell him I'd come?'

B.J. said yes with her eyebrows; she raised them once.

'You're an absolute bloody fool!'

Heather knew the insanity of refusing to see the D.E.O., especially after B.J. had promised. He was the only person who could make life difficult for her and she had already made up her mind that she would apply for a transfer back to Nairobi as soon as the term ended. The District Education Officer would have to approve that transfer.

And now in the bar of the Horse and Hunter Wilbur was looking at her closely and saying, 'I don't know *your* name either.'

His whole face was in sharp contrast to Heather's. It was more than a simple colour opposite; his tight thick skin shone in the unshaded bar-bulbs. It was perfectly smooth, his whole head rounded, the dome a tonsure edged with a thin wreath of black fuzz. His knobbed nose gaped hairlessly, while two ivory wedges of front tooth protruded into his wide soft lips. He stared hugely at Heather in a slightly crouching position (she was sitting), his neck shortened and swollen in almost tie-bursting tension. He seemed to Heather like a black rubber monster, life-sized, that some infantile practical joker had inflated and stuck with her in the small room.

Heather's sharp narrow-nostrilled beak trembled menacingly at Wilbur. Her lips were daubed in the usual red bow, but the red had rubbed from the place her lips met. The sutures of her bony forehead showed under the slack facial skin which, very pale, was covered with tiny blonde powder-caked hairs. She said, 'My name is Heather Monk-house.'

'That's good,' said Wilbur, and he repeated to himself, 'Heather Monkhouse.' He went back to the bar and ordered more drinks for everyone, including Fitch. Then he turned towards Heather and said, 'Miss Heather Monk-house, are you a teacher?'

'That is correct,' said Heather coldly, accepting her gin. 'I'm down the road at the girls' school.'

'At the girls' school,' said Wilbur thoughtfully, wrinkling his face.

'She teaches English and drama,' said B.J. 'They won't let us Americans teach English. On account of we ain't speaking it so hot!' she added comically.

'So you *are* a Yank,' said Fitch to B.J.

'Yes, I am,' said B.J. uneasily, sipping at her beer.

'But you said –'

'I had amnesia.'

'You had a fooking bad case of it, to my way of thinking,' said Fitch, scratching himself.

'Miss Heather,' said Wilbur, who had neither drunk his whisky nor taken his eyes off Heather, 'were you ever by any chance in Nairobi?'

Heather wondered whether she should answer, then remembered that she was talking to the District Education Officer. It was futile to lie; all the files were in his office. 'Yes,' she said, 'I was transferred here at the beginning of the term.'

'So was I,' said Wilbur, forming a smile. 'I was an Assistant D.E.O. in Nairobi.'

'Nairobi is like Omaha,' said B.J. to Wangi.

'That's inter*est*ing,' Wangi replied, drunkenly stressing the third syllable. He swallowed the last watery drops of his whisky and handed his glass to Fitch for a refill.

ked Nairobi,' said Heather.

ghtening everyone, Wilbur burst out laughing. His rumbling laughter seemed to shake the black-framed watercolours of game fish that covered the bar walls. He woke the dogs, who immediately began howling, then stopped when he did. 'I know *you*,' he said to Heather. 'I remember *your* case.' He laughed again; giggle-borne tears welled in his eyes.

B.J. saw Heather stiffen; she feared Heather might do something nasty, call Wilbur an insulting name. Heather appeared to be thinking rapidly; her lips were moving as if going over all the possible alternatives. And then her whole body relaxed, she forced a smile, put her drink down and said, 'Why don't you come over here next to me, Wilbur?' She patted the bench with the tips of her fingers.

'Heather Monkhouse,' said Wilbur, pointing a large joshing finger into Heather's face, 'your case was a *good* one!'

'Come here,' said Heather almost seductively.

It worked like a charm. Wilbur sat down and put his left arm around Heather's neck. His whisky was in his left hand. When he drank he bumped Heather's face with his forearm. Heather smiled bravely.

'Do they know?' asked Wilbur, tossing his head in the direction of B.J. and Wangi.

'Shh,' Heather hushed; she whispered, 'Not here. We'll talk about it later.' She affectionately pinched the mischief out of Wilbur's face and rose. 'The same for everyone – a double for Wilbur,' she called to Fitch.

Wilbur grinned and shook his head from side to side.

'I'll never understand you fooking lot,' Fitch muttered across the bar at Heather.

Heather passed the drinks and returned to her seat next to Wilbur. She told a long story in the B.B.C. voice that she had learned since coming to Africa, shushing interruptions as she proceeded by saying, 'You said you were all for integration, so let me finish.' The story was of a marriage that had taken place two years before between a former teacher at Miss Poole's school, an Englishwoman, and the Provincial Commissioner, an African. They married shortly after the woman arrived in East Africa; she was said to have learned Swahili in record time; she wore wax-print sarongs, ate local stews and had amassed a huge collection of drums and digging sticks in her house. She had met the Provincial Commissioner at a native *baraza* (he had just returned from a short course in England). They fell in love and were married in a village ceremony: there was much feasting and drumming. She resigned her job at the school and took to pounding peanuts in a mortar at the back of the house. Less than six months later the African announced that he had quit his job in the civil service and was making plans to emigrate to England. The woman was distressed; she refused to go. There were arguments that ended in fistfights. The woman was admitted to the local hospital with a broken wrist and severe bruises on her face. A divorce followed. The woman moved farther up-country, nearly to the frontier where she lived in a village with an illiterate tribesman, gave birth to a coffee-coloured child and let herself grow fat. The ex-husband, the African who had beat her, left for England. It was said that he had just married – this, the latest instalment – a woman of his own tribe who lived in Ealing.

B.J. said that the Englishwoman would eventually go back to England. 'She *has* to. Her family's there, aren't they?'

'Suppose she had no family?' Heather asked. 'Suppose they're all dead?'

'England is bloody dead,' said Fitch. 'What with the

beastly bloody cold and the fooking socialists and the dirty great factories and the queers and fairies and what not, England is bloody dead.'

'Yeah, but she can't stay here, can she?' said B.J. 'I mean, she's English, isn't she?'

'Are you planning to stay here?' Wilbur asked Heather.

'You want teachers, don't you? Who would teach the girls at the school if I went? Africans don't like being teachers. They want to be Prime Ministers, ha-ha. Of course I'm staying,' said Heather smiling, her head swaying, heavy with gin.

'Are *you*?' Wilbur turned to B.J.

'No *sir*!' said B.J. emphatically. And then she remembered Wangi. He sighed into his glass. 'That is,' she swallowed, 'I don't *think* I am. It's not that I don't like it here – it's great, really. But, well, to be perfectly honest, I thought Africa was different. Or something like that. But that's not why I'm going. Even if Africa was like what I thought it was, but it wasn't, I'd still be going back ... golly, everybody's got to go home some time, haven't they?'

She looked at Wangi. His face was impassive. 'Haven't they?' she asked again. Wangi looked away. Heather smirked.

'Drink up,' said Fitch thickly. 'It's time.'

16
Blackmail

A moonscape appeared: crippled, twisted cacti, ant-hills, dry crater basins, and round bare mounds like inverted bowls, all of these frosted with ghostly silver and hard and darkened at ground level. On the far horizon was a black irregular fence of mountains. It was as if they were bumping across the moon in an old-fashioned rocket-ship; B.J. imagined the Africans two dark streamlined moonmen, one at the controls, the other seated silently next to her as the rickety machine was guided through the dramatic bareness in the unearthly gleam. Africa was much weirder at night.

The car plunged down a grade full-tilt and shot into a forest, leaving the moonscape behind. Desert turns to forest in East Africa without warning, arid plains become dank swamp, and sometimes snowy peaks show over the banana groves. Now a rotting dampness chilled the car; all the deep-green trees and vines seemed soaked, dense with lushness and oozing jungly waters. From the thick shadows, glowing animal eyes appeared, shone for seconds and then were gone. And owls, perched in the centre of the road, flushed noisily into the air with a wind-rush of big slow wings as the car passed, the beating wings brushing the upper part of the windshield. The headlights of the rocking car made all the great boulders, tree-trunks and ferns dance past in a frantic conga of rubbery twitching shapes.

When they reached the asphalt road, Wilbur speeded up;

the tyres crackled, popping open the fallen jacaranda blossoms which quilted the road. Inside the school compound Wilbur slowed the car to a crawl. He drove cautiously past Miss Poole's to Heather's, where he coasted to a halt and cranked up the hand-brake, leaving the engine still ticking.

'Thank you so much,' said Heather. 'It's been fun.'

'It sure has,' said B.J., sitting up in the back seat.

Heather started to lift the door-handle.

'Miss Heather,' said Wilbur, 'would you mind if I used your *facilities*? I think I'm going to burst if I don't find a latrine.' He chuckled softly.

'I'd rather you didn't,' said Heather.

'I *will* burst!'

'I'd rather you didn't come in.'

'Are you afraid I'll stand on the seat?'

'It's late,' said Heather impatiently. 'Couldn't you just do it in the garden?'

'You think I'm a savage, don't you?' The joviality had left Wilbur. His eyes flashed white at Heather in the darkness of the car. A panel light illuminated his large hand, nothing more.

'Of course not,' Heather protested. 'I just –'

Wilbur jerked his door open and got out. 'Take this little girl to her house, Wangi,' he said. Then he walked to Heather's side of the car and, with an effort, got her door open; it had not been fixed since the time Wangi went off the back road. Wangi got out and made his way to the driver's seat.

Before Heather got out of the car B.J. leaned forward and touched her shoulder. In a whisper she said, 'I don't think Wangi's too crazy about my leaving and everything. He hasn't said one word since we left the bar – hey, do you think he's okay?'

'I wouldn't know,' said Heather with a coldness in her voice that B.J. had never heard before.

'Look, I know this was my idea, but I think I said the wrong – please, Heather, *wait* –' The door slammed. Heather disappeared.

B.J. got into the front seat. Wangi shifted the car roughly into gear and drove up the road, past the servants' quarters, to the small school bungalow where B.J. lived with Miss Male. What alarmed B.J. was that there were no lights burning in the house.

'It's through there,' said Heather in the living-room, pointing vaguely to a darkened hallway. She did not look at Wilbur. 'First door on the left.'

She sat on the edge of the sofa and pressed her hands to her eyes. She tried not to hear the relentless cataract bubbling grossly into the bowl, then the dripping, a hawking of phlegm, the silly tinkle of the chain, the loud flush and glug. But she heard it all, her drunkenness amplifying and distorting the ugly sounds, as if it was happening three feet away. She wanted to rush into her bedroom and lock the door, to hide until Wilbur discovered her gone and went away himself. She rose to do this – she could not think of anything else to do – but as she did, Wilbur entered the room buttoning the jacket of his suit across his pot belly.

'Miss Heather Monkhouse,' said Wilbur with a crooked smile, looking Heather straight in the eye.

'I wish you'd stop saying that,' said Heather. She walked to the front door and stood with her hand on the doorknob. Delicate white moths had collected on the outside of the screen; they crept around in circles, fluttering their wings, watching the light with large eyes.

'Why, Miss Heather Monkhouse?'

'I'm sick of hearing you say it. I don't think you're very amusing.'

'It's your name, isn't it?'

Heather did not respond.

'I said, it's your name –'

'Yes, it's my bloody name. So what?'

'Monkhouse,' said Wilbur. 'Is that English?'

'Stop it. Of course it is.'

'I was in England, you know. Aberystwyth.'

'That's in Wales.'

'Yes, Wales. You English are more tribal than we Africans.'

'Rubbish,' said Heather. 'Wales is a different place.'

'So is Africa.'

'So it is.'

'You like it here?'

'What if I do?'

'I'm simply asking.'

'Sometimes I like it. But you –' She paused; she wondered whether she should say *blacks* or *Africans* '– you Africans think you own the whole place.'

'We do own it. It's our country.'

'Then you come to England and think you own England, too. What a cheeky lot!'

'We paid for England. You exploited us and stole –'

'We *worked* here and built this country and you damned well better believe it. This was all ours once, all of this –'

'Miss Heather Monkhouse,' Wilbur sneered.

'Stop saying my name!' The African was mocking her, an African mouth saying her name over and over again. She wanted to crush his insolent face.

'A very neat little house,' said Wilbur fingering an ash-tray that had been made from the hoof of an animal. He strolled casually around the living-room picking up magazines, looking at the spines of books on the shelf, the framed photograph on the desk. 'Nice things. From England?'

'Isn't it time you went home?' Heather said, as rudely as she could.

'No. I'm not ready yet. I want to talk to you.' Wilbur glanced up from a magazine he had been leafing through and leered at Heather.

'I don't want to talk to *you*. Don't think you can barge in here and insult me just because you're an education officer and I'm a teacher. You have no right. I can call the police.'

'Call them,' Wilbur said. 'Do you think they'll believe anything you say? Don't forget, we Africans are all brothers.'

'You Africans cut each other's throats, don't tell me you don't.'

'Your throat maybe,' Wilbur said, 'but not my brother's.' He played with an ivory letter-opener.

Heather became frightened: he *could* cut her throat, very easily. She changed her tone. 'I'm very tired. Please go. I have to work tomorrow.'

'Tomorrow is Saturday.'

'This is a boarding school. We have to work every day. You should know that. You're an education officer.'

'Yes, I am,' said Wilbur. 'I was an education officer in Nairobi, too.'

Heather glanced at her wrist-watch. 'See here,' she said, 'it's after twelve –'

'When you were in Nairobi, that's when I was there,' Wilbur cackled. He grinned as he had done in the Horse and Hunter when he first learned her name, and again he said, 'I remember your case.'

Heather crouched in a chair some distance from Wilbur,

167

who had seated himself on the sofa. She took a breath and then spoke. 'That's quite enough,' she said. 'I've had enough of this. It was damned inconsiderate of you to bring that up while we were there at the bar with those others listening. What happened in Nairobi is over and done with. In any case, it's my affair, not yours. I don't want to hear about it again and I don't want the people here to start talking about it. You should be thankful I didn't row with you in the bar when you brought it up, but if you insist on taunting me with my name and gloating over what you know about me, I shall make a scene here and you'll be sorry. Mark me, you'll regret ever talking to me and you'll rue the bloody day you came here to piss. Your superiors wouldn't like it if they knew you were in my house making my life a misery —'

Wilbur interrupted her harangue by shouting, 'What would *your* superiors,' he gasped, 'your superiors say if they knew about you?' Wilbur was rattled.

'I daresay they bloody well know!' Heather brayed.

'I'll tell them about the police station. I was there at the police station after you made that big *shauri* at that fellow's house —'

'Shut your mouth! Leave my house this instant,' Heather said through clenched teeth.

'I'll leave when I feel like it,' said Wilbur. He walked heavily towards Heather. 'You're a Boer. This isn't your country. You have no business —'

'Get out, you insolent bastard. You filthy . . .' Heather choked; racial abuse, every vile name she could think of, welled in her throat; the words trembled there, already formed. Now she would let him have it; she wanted him to know how much she hated him. She tried to select the most offensive words, but Wilbur had already started shouting back.

'Don't talk to me that way – I'm not your houseboy. I know a lot about you. If you make me angry I could just go ahead and tell anyone about you.'

'That's blackmail!'

'Don't say that to me,' Wilbur hissed. He started for her, but Heather stepped back. 'I'll get you and no one will know about it. You can't scream loud enough. You're not in Nairobi now.'

'Stay where you are!' Heather snatched a large glass ashtray and flung it; it sang past Wilbur's head and hit the far wall. It did not break, but the clang it made stopped Wilbur. He was near the desk, huge with rage. He slammed his fist down on the desk so hard that the framed photograph flew off and tumbled to the floor.

'You're a blackmailer!'

'Shut up!' snarled Wilbur. 'What have you got against black people?'

'I hate you, I hate you,' Heather said in sincere, almost prayerful ejaculations, as she backed towards the opening to the hallway. She saw that Wilbur had misunderstood, and she was glad; it could not have been better if she had actually said all the words that had run through her mind a few moments earlier. He faced her, raging, his mouth hanging open.

'We're as good as you are. I've had English girls, plenty of them –'

'*Welsh* girls, more likely!' Heather laughed hysterically and stepped back again.

'They loved me,' Wilbur said, crossing the floor, stooped and swaying like a drunken bear. 'They loved me.'

'I *hate* you!' Heather saw the words wound him; Wilbur made two large black fists and lifted them at her. Heather spun, skidded down the hallway to her room, banged the door and locked it. At the last click of the key she heard

169

a muffled thump in the living-room, as if Wilbur's body was hitting the solid floor. Then there was a deep sigh.

In the darkness of her bedroom, Heather's heart pounded; she could feel it pulsing hatefully against her throat. She pressed the side of her head to the door to hear Wilbur, but heard only herself, all the pumping noises of fear and anger from her own body, her heart, her blood, her rapid breath. She stayed in the room for what seemed to her a long while. Still hearing nothing, she went to the window and looked out. She could see some tall silvery trees, the glistening grass, some neat rows of flowerbeds; there was no movement, although she suspected that she might be startled by Wilbur clawing at her window. Nothing outside moved: it could have been a winter scene, the whole landscape frozen into stillness by the cold moon.

She went to the door again and listened, her ear against the wood. Her heart had slowed and she was no longer panting; several minutes passed in the fuzzy faraway engine-hum of the deep silence. Turning the key slowly so that it would not click, she unlocked the door, twisted the knob and edged the door noiselessly open. When she peeked into the hallway, she could see one of Wilbur's feet, toes pointing upward, protruding into the hallway. She tiptoed towards him and took a long look: Wilbur was stretched out, mouth gaping open, on his back; his belly swelled obscenely, arms in a welcoming gesture of either lust or anger. Beside him lay the small framed photograph (Heather in a straw hat at Brighton, aged six); the glass was cracked where Wilbur's heel had crushed it and slipped.

At that moment, with the photograph in her hand, Heather heard a sharp sound at the front door. She turned quickly in panic and saw Rufus, his nose pressed into the screen, pawing the doorframe and growling softly.

'This is a fine time to show up,' Heather said with a

shiver. Rufus howled when he saw Wilbur. Heather pulled him by the collar into her bedroom; with Rufus there she knew she would be perfectly safe.

Heather could not tell if Wilbur was breathing, she could not bear to put her face close enough to find out – a whisky-reek hung about his head that, worse than suggesting drunkenness, made him seem a dead monster shot with the alcoholic preservative that keeps large specimens whole. She lifted out a piece of the shattered picture-glass from the little frame and held this shard across his lips. A small moist cloud collected on the glass.

The swine, Heather thought. And with this thought came a feeling of terrible remoteness and smallness: she was trapped in a little house with a black unconscious man, in a little post, late at night, as far away from help and sanity as one could ever get. There was nothing to do but to lock him in the spare bedroom; in the morning, gagged with a hangover, in blinding sunlight, he would weakly go away, she hoped.

From her bedroom Heather got a rectangular carpet. She spread it beside the body and, by twisting his legs, rolled Wilbur on to the carpet on his face. The floor was smooth waxed concrete under the sisal mats; Heather kicked the mats aside and with a great effort tugged the carpet – Wilbur lying the length of it – into the spare-room.

Heather was in bed when she remembered Wangi. She had to go all the way to her front door, with Rufus in tow, to get a glimpse of B.J.'s house. Across the moon-silvered meadow she could just make out the car. It was parked under a tree, dead-still and gleaming with starry dew. There were no lights on in the car or in B.J.'s house.

'Stupid girl,' muttered Heather. She put out all the lights, locked all the doors and went to bed, remembering to lock her own bedroom door and wedge a chairback against the knob. She was aware of Wilbur's presence two locked rooms away, as if he were giving off a sickening odour of decay. He was there in her small house, inert on his back, a huge dark carcass, like the image of the putrefying black devil she had once had of the whole continent.

17
'Can I See You?'

Heather blundered into troubled sleep and towards dawn had a nightmare. She was on a photographic safari in a Congo forest with several other women she thought she knew. They had all been warned against going so deep into the forest without a male guide; all the women were afraid except Heather, who mocked their fear by parodying their whining voices. After dinner the women sat around a fire and talked about the giant gorillas that lived in the area. As they spoke, Heather looked up and in the flickering of the fire saw five rubber-faced creatures, as big as houses, lumbering erect into the clearing. The women screamed and ran in all directions, upsetting pots and spilling water on the fire. Heather could not move at first; the gorillas were bearing down on her. She rose from her canvas chair in slow motion and grasped the trunk of a tall tree which she climbed with aching delay, looking down at the gorillas at the bottom. When she reached the tree-top she clung breathlessly to a flimsy branch and sensed a shadow moving across her, blocking the starlight. Craning her neck back she saw, towering above her, a sixth slavering gorilla, a King Kong hundreds of feet tall, his arms stretched wide, fingers apart, about to embrace her.

There was a stiff rapping at the front door. Sunlight dispersed the nightmare like flames destroying a photograph. Heather jumped out of bed. As she put on her robe she glanced at her watch: five past eight. Rufus snored in the corner. Still dazed with the terror of the nightmare, she clumsily unlocked the bedroom door and stumbled in the direction of the knocking. With the bedroom door open, the knocking was very loud; it woke Rufus, who began barking at the door of the spare-room, then leaping and scratching at it.

'Quiet *down*, Rufus,' Heather said. To the rapping door Heather called, 'All *right*, I'm coming.'

She slid the bolt and saw the faded woollen beret, the blotched face; Rose was standing close to the threshold as an intrusive salesman or beggar might do. In the sunlight Heather could pick out every vein in the pale skin; Rose's snub nose was sunburned, white skin-flakes peeled petal-like from her face and arms, exposing thin chafed skin. The dark eyeless goggles faced Heather and mirrored Heather's blue robe. Rose stuck her hand out.

'Letter from Memsab.'

Heather took the letter and closed the door on Rose's face. She ripped a thin strip from the side of the envelope and took out a small sheet of paper. There was very little writing on it, without a signature but in Miss Poole's hand: *Please come to my office at once. Urgent matter to discuss.*

'Damn her,' Heather said aloud; she crumpled the letter into a ball and flung it at the wastebasket. And then she heard Rufus barking in the hall. She rushed to the door of the spare-room and listened, as if all at once there would be a roar inside the room or the thumping of Wilbur's fists on the door. There was no sound except Rufus moaning and scratching.

'You'll wake him up, won't you?' Heather whispered to the dog. She took him by the collar and dragged him out of the house; Rufus continued to strain in the direction of the spare-room, imploring with his moans, his shuttling

body and waggling tail. 'Better come with me, old boy.'
Heather locked the front door.

'Please take a pew, Miss Monkhouse,' said Miss Poole.
She spoke lightly, but seemed nervous; she was shuffling
papers on her desk to disguise the trembling of her hands.
'There is something I wish to discuss with you.'

'I gathered as much,' said Heather. She was not interested in annoying Miss Poole and was not even aware
that for the first time ever Miss Poole was speaking
courteously to her. Even the thought of Wilbur left her
momentarily, for as soon as she had spoken and looked at
Miss Poole's face, the details of her dream returned. Miss
Poole, Heather now realized, had been one of the women
in the camp and had been the first to run when the hairy
creatures entered the clearing. Miss Poole had run quickly;
she seemed to know an escape-route, but of course she had
been running deeper into the jungle. Like most dreams,
Heather decided, it was about sex. She had read her Freud;
with D. H. Lawrence he was one of the two male writers
Heather took seriously. Both had 'terrifying insight' – the
phrase was a reviewer's, Heather had seen it on a Lawrence paperback – into women's desires and, curiously,
both had the woman's gift of frank sensitivity. And they
both wrote about sex. Heather believed that any writer who
was concerned with women and ignored sex was a fool, for
there was no race, no nation or person who had normal sex.
Her dream was clear to her and it contained a warning: the
tumescent male apes, the women scattering, screaming
into the tall trees. The warning would have to be heeded.
Heather searched the dream for further phallicism and
resolved to get herself laid at the earliest opportunity,
either anonymously or for old times' sake, with a good
friend.

Miss Poole was talking about the school, rambling on about duties, the Head Girl, what the prefects were saying about the hockey team – all of it without malice. But Heather was not listening; she was thinking of a hotel on the beach at Mombasa: she was naked in a darkened room, near a window which opened on to palm trees and surf; she was joking with a bare-chested man who sat on the edge of a four-poster untying his shoes. She would do it. If any arguments were needed for doing it, they could be read on the face of the woman gabbing aimlessly behind the desk. Miss Poole's was a face illustrating extreme fatigue, paranoia, bush-fever, and other symptoms of dry anxiety; it was the unretouched photograph of the *News of the World* crackpot, blurred somewhat by the bad lighting but otherwise described fully in the caption: note heavy lids, compressed lips, dull hair, vacant eyes set in dark circles, sallow malnourished complexion, shrivelled neck. Sitting there talking to Heather in pointless syllables, staring while nervously fidgeting, arranging loose papers into neat piles with her fingertips, Miss Poole looked to Heather as if she were being gnawed at from within by a large worm.

'This is the end of term,' Miss Poole was saying.

'I am aware of that,' said Heather, thinking, *A real dirty time I'll have for myself, some swimming, the sun, a man. If I can't have a husband, I'll have the next best thing; and who knows, it might be better than a husband?*

'I've been doing quite a bit of work, sorting out schedules and so forth. The exams, um ...' Miss Poole continued, almost as if she were purposely delaying Heather, glancing past Heather to the door as she prattled on. 'The exams will be in about a week's time –'

'Exams,' said Heather coming awake and thinking, for the first time since she entered the office, thoughts of Wilbur. 'Yes. Well,' said Heather distractedly, 'if you're asking my opinion I'd say flatly no, don't bother.'

'No? I don't think you understand –'

'It is *because* I understand that I'm saying no. Exams for these girls can't possibly do any earthly good. Now I really must be off . . .'

Miss Poole stopped arranging papers on her desk and drew back from Heather. The movement made Heather pause; Miss Poole's face continued to remind Heather of a woman with a grave illness. Miss Poole said, 'May I ask what you mean by that?'

'Tell me, Miss Poole, if one of the girls fails her exams, will you send her back to her village?'

'If a girl fails, she'll have to pull her socks up, and smartly. You know that.'

'I know that I've been through these so-called exams hundreds of times. They're a bloody farce – we had them in Nairobi at Mainwaring and I know we'll have them here. But if you're asking my opinion on the matter, as I believe you are doing, then I will tell you how useless I think they are. Girls who fail their exams stay on at the school like everyone else, like a bunch of bloody –'

'You mean to say that you're concerned about the academic standards at this school?'

'In my way,' said Heather curtly.

'I would hardly have thought so from your behaviour.'

'My behaviour, as you call it, is my business.'

'We were talking about exams,' said Miss Poole.

'See here,' said Heather, raising her voice, 'I am a teacher, whatever you may think of me, and I feel every responsibility for what happens at this filthy school. Or *fails* to happen. I have never in my life –'

'I would have thought differently,' said Miss Poole, a cold angry light coming into her eyes.

'Oh, you would, would you?' Heather chattered, but her

mind was on Wilbur. Each time she thought of him and jerked forward to leave, Miss Poole delayed her. 'You've spent a good part of the school term on sick leave, Miss Poole. You forget that I have had a great deal to do with the day-to-day running of this place in your absence.'

'I haven't forgotten that,' Miss Poole said with hatred.

'I'm pleased to hear –'

'Oh, yes,' Miss Poole went on, 'I see what you've done. I have noted our numerous disasters.'

'Disasters? *Which* disasters?'

'You know very well what I mean,' said Miss Poole, touching at her sallow face as if she had become conscious that there was something wrong with it, as if she was developing a defensive mannerism to hide it, like the person with bad teeth who learns not to grin.

'I have no idea what you're talking about.'

Miss Poole itemized in a high voice: 'The girls' utter disregard for authority, the chronic lateness and lack of discipline, the wanton destruction of the laboratory and the library annexe. And many other things, all terrible, all since you arrived at this compound.'

Heather's eyes widened. 'I do believe you're mad, Miss Poole. I used to think you were a nasty-minded old bitch, but you're not – you're stark staring bonkers!'

'I know you want to think that,' said Miss Poole, her voice breaking. 'You want to think that and you've been telling everyone around here –'

'Everyone? There's *no one* around here!'

'You've been spreading lies about me so that I'll be forced to resign. And I know why – you want to be me!'

'*That's a bloody lie*,' Heather blurted, rising from her chair. She was frightened by the words; they were a kind of truthful prophecy, based on logic, as the dream had been, reversible but also possible. Heather knew that in a few years, if she took no precautions and let herself be guided by Africa's bestial nudges, it could very easily come about: she, Heather, would be the mad Headmistress rotting away in the bush girls' school. With venom, as if to poison Miss Poole's words, she spat out, 'I don't want to be *you*!'

'I didn't mean that,' said Miss Poole sadly. 'I meant that you want to be Headmistress. I know you do.'

'I most certainly do not,' Heather said disgustedly. She walked to the door and said, 'I had planned to tell you this week, but you might as well know it now. This is the bush, as far as I'm concerned, and it's going to stay that way. I'm leaving. I intend to leave this school as soon as the term ends and never come back. Good day.' She banged the door.

From her cool stone office Miss Poole peered out of the window at Heather crossing the grass. The sun beat down and whitened Heather's skin to a ghostliness that in East Africa gave the expatriates a look of special strangeness. Heather's whole being bleached and seemed to lighten and get nastier from the sun's intense rays; when she reached the road to her house she sent up a puff of dust with each step – such an odd figure, so unearthly among the emerald green of the grass and trees, the wild reds and yellows of the flowers, a devilish intruder with shapeless ectoplasmic body, moving across the fresh green like a slug on a track of slime. '*Liar*,' said Miss Poole.

When the word settled on her tongue there was a *clank* at the office door. Miss Poole spun around but became calm when she saw who it was stepping over the threshold: Rose, head tilted shyly down, one arm extended, and in her scabby hand a bunch of keys.

'I want to talk to you,' called Miss Male. She hurried rubber-sandalled across the grass towards Heather.

Heather had placed her hand on the door-knob, but withdrew it quickly when she heard the voice. She did not want to invite Miss Male in; she could imagine the scene: a loud banging on the spare-room door while Miss Male sat bewildered in the living-room, then shouting from the locked-in Wilbur, accusations possibly, howling, a noisy row. She put her back to the door and, like a sentry, faced Miss Male.

'What is it?' He might be shuffling around the locked room, he could be forcing the door or prising the burglar bars from the windows. Fortunately – as far as Heather could make out it was the only fortunate thing in a morning of misfortune – the spare-room was at the back of the house.

'Can I see you? It's rather urgent.' Miss Male was out of breath.

'I've just had a frightful *shauri* with the Memsab. I'm on my way back to bed – don't tell me you've got problems, too.' Heather tried to be gay, but her gaiety missed and she sounded even more gruff than she was.

'Not me,' said Miss Male, shielding the sun from her eyes with her hand cupped to the side of her head. She proceeded, squinting gravely, 'It's B.J. I'm terribly worried about her. I think she's poorly.'

'I'm sure it's nothing. Now if you'll excuse me –'

'Listen, please,' Miss Male begged. 'She's been sobbing in her room since early this morning. She refuses to talk to me or get out of bed.'

'Why should she get up? It's Saturday. If I hadn't got an urgent note from that bitch this morning I'd be in bed, too, I can tell you.'

'But it's not *like* her to go on this way. Please help me – I don't know what to do.'

'Don't do a thing,' said Heather. She made a gesture with

her shoulders to signal that the subject was closed as far as she was concerned. Miss Male did not move.

'I'm very worried. I –'

'If you don't mind my saying so, Pam, you're not being very sporting about this.'

'You don't seem to realize that this is a serious –'

'I realize *perfectly*,' Heather exploded. She stopped and resumed in a softer tone, calmly and reasonably, as if talking to a child: 'I realize perfectly what has happened.'

'I don't think you do, Heather.'

'No one,' said Heather, 'gives me credit for knowing anything that goes on around here. It's fantastic. I've been at this school nearly a whole term and I am putting it to you – and mind you, I said the same thing to the Memsab ten minutes ago – that I *do* know, about B.J. and everything else in this bloody compound. My advice is to leave the girl alone.' Again Heather reached for the door-knob, again Miss Male stood firm.

'She's been crying her heart out.'

'And so she should,' said Heather crossly.

Miss Male looked at Heather as if at a stranger. 'You don't know what you're saying.'

'Oh, I *do*!' Heather laughed mirthlessly.

'That's cruel of you, Heather. That poor girl –'

'That poor girl,' Heather mocked. 'That poor girl – Pamela, isn't it about time you learned the facts of life?'

'I would like to know what you mean by that remark,' said Miss Male, blushing in anger.

'Just that. You're getting upset for nothing. Do you by any chance know where your Yankee friend was last night?'

'I didn't see her. I went to bed.'

'Didn't she tell you where she was going?'

'She said for a drink.'

'For a drink. Shall I tell you where she was, what she did?'

Miss Male pressed her lips together. She watched Heather.

'Well, I'll tell you. She had a date with her silent little African friend, the piccanin from the Electricity Board. I went along to see they stayed out of trouble, but of course I can't be everywhere. At about midnight they dropped me here. Just before I went to bed I happened to look out the window and saw a car parked near your house – not too close, you understand, but near enough. Now you tell me she's in bed weeping – this, the morning after I saw the car. I put one and one together and decide that your friend B.J. was getting thoroughly screwed, pardon my French, in the back seat –'

Miss Male bit her lip and frowned, as if she was the one who had been speaking and had abruptly stopped. 'If I had only stayed up and waited for her.'

'If you had stayed up I doubt that you could have done a thing.'

'Why, you act as if she *wanted* to do that . . . that –'

'Don't be a fool – of course she wanted to. These things don't have to happen. Rape is biologically impossible, don't you know that?' As Heather spoke she thought again of Wilbur, apishly caged in the spare-room, preparing to bellow wildly through his rubber mouth or, bulked against the frail door, about to break it noisily to splinters.

'He looks quite a strong chap.'

'Who does?' Heather saw only Wilbur.

'B.J.'s friend.'

'Rubbish. Tell me honestly, Pam, have you ever been raped?'

'No, in fact I never –'

'I haven't either and I've been in Africa for some little

time. I don't believe in rape. There's no such thing. Oh, there were lots of times when I wanted desperately to believe that it had been rape – with me, you know. But it wasn't, it couldn't have been. The odds are against the rapist.'

'Are you saying –'

'I am saying that I have seen these girls before. They come here looking for it – it's the big liberal thing, you know, opening your legs in Africa. Talk to the drivers in the tour-buses, ask them, *they* know. Did you know that these American tourists, those old hags you see dressed up in topees and bush jackets – did you know that at night they crawl into the buses and bed down with the drivers? It's true. I have a friend in Nairobi who's a travel agent. He told me. The drivers love it.'

'That doesn't explain B.J. Whatever you may think of her, I can tell you she isn't mad on Africans. She's dying to leave.'

'It doesn't make any difference. You forget that we're free, we girls. We can do anything we want. Look,' said Heather, gesturing around the garden and flapping her hand in the direction of the boggy meadow, the clumps of shiny bamboos with their sprays of narrow leaves, 'we're single, and here we are in Africa. We came all this distance alone – the whole place is ours. And that's what's wrong with us. We're as bad as Africans – we're ashamed to admit that we want something simple.'

'Something simple?'

'A man,' Heather said, 'a husband. What fool wants to be single? I'd take any man I could lay my hands on, providing he was white.'

Miss Male kicked at a lump of dirt near her feet, a small mound; the top of the mound crumbled and revealed a black smooth-sided hole swarming with fleeing ants.

'Poor B.J.,' said Miss Male. She had taken her hand from the side of her face and was letting the sun shine into her eyes, into her whole helpless face.

'She'll get over it. Oh, she'll moan for a few days, but she'll sort things out. She got what she wanted. Now I must go.'

Miss Male said nothing more. She turned and walked away, across the grass, towards her house. She walked slowly, dejectedly hunched, watching her sandals flap. She did not look back.

The front door was unlocked, but Heather could not remember if she had locked it when she went out or, indeed, if she had unlocked it before Miss Male held her up. She entered the house and, the moment she did, sensed something was wrong; things seemed out of place enough to nudge the senses without being absolutely scattered. When she entered the hall she saw the door to the spare-room half-open. The room was empty, sunshine streamed through the window. Where Wilbur had been lying there was a damp stain, a gamy odour of stale breath. Then Rufus appeared – from nowhere with a bound, his tongue drooping – and began barking. But he was barking only at the odour, for the house was empty.

18
Incubus

It was so dark, the girl's voice was so soft: she appeared, a figment in a rag of light, at the far corner of B.J.'s bedroom. Not B.J. herself, but a girl B.J. seemed to know well, one she thought she recognized, had seen many times before and was on the point of naming when, distracted by the girl's helplessness, the girl's identity became unimportant. She did not need a name. She was being raped.

It seemed a cramped waste-area of edges and moony light there in the corner of the room; the girl was on her back, twisted uncomfortably and softly pleading. It went on all Saturday and then into Sunday, the blinds drawn in her room, the girl appearing at a distance which made all B.J.'s efforts to dispel the vision futile, like the nagging dirty beggar who will not go away, who keeps his distance and wails open-faced, motioning towards his mouth, asking for bread. The awful repeating vision of the girl being attacked seemed provoked by the aches in B.J.'s body; her own pain induced pain.

On Sunday night the bodies and voices came again, as they had come a hundred times, all the words now familiar, ordered, shaping themselves in an aching pattern. This insistent rehearsal of shadow and panic shuddering there on the wall made B.J. moan, for the more times she heard it and saw it, the clearer the separate actions became; she anticipated each violent gesture. The girl's pain hurt B.J., and the only way B.J. could get relief from it was to sob as loudly as she could. At times she managed to freeze the progress of the vision by yelling, '*Stop!*' And she found she could slow it by crying. But when she was silent, it began again with dreadful sameness, proceeding with horrifying and deliberate efficiency, increasing in clarity as the rag of light spread over the wall; now it was two people, a girl and a silvery black man occupying the far wall of her room.

'Now what?' The girl spoke in what appeared to be the stuffy darkness of a car's front seat.

The black man said nothing. His head was unsteady; he slowly swung it around to face the girl.

'Look, I've got to go,' the girl drawled.

The black man placed his hand on the girl's shoulder. When the girl shuddered and pulled away, the black man slid close and held her with two hands.

'Stop it,' the girl said, but she did not say it loudly; it was a teacher's reprimand. She tried to get loose; she squirmed; there was not enough room on the front seat to move about in. The black man was close, like an insect in a hairy suit, bulbous-eyed, with long flicking arms and sticky gripping fingers. He did not speak; he held the girl and pressed himself against her.

'Would you please cut it out!' The girl got one of her arms free and reached for the door-handle.

Without taking his face away from her neck the black man seized her arm roughly and, when he felt it, punched down hard against her forearm, knocking it limp.

'Ow, that *hurt*!' The pain was unexpected; it worried the girl and made her examine what was happening to her. The black man was holding her tightly; his weight pressed her down on the seat; her legs seemed to be sliding forward and she could not move her left arm, which was wedged at her side by the pressure of the black man's body. The musky smell of sweat and breath crowded into her nose and mouth; and then, as the smell grew stronger, the girl felt a hand on top of her head, fingers reaching as far down as her ears like a grotesque cap, shoving her down.

Here B.J. screamed, but she was weak and could not make the vision pause. She hated this part of it; it terrified her as nothing else had ever done, and in this terror she was flooded with nausea which made it impossible to end the vision or escape it. For this fleeting moment B.J. felt everything the girl felt, each sensation of touch, the black fingers pinioning the girl, the breath on her, the weight of the man. B.J. crouched in her bed with her face against her knees: again it was happening.

It was this. A soft strand in the girl's body refused to resist the man; she thought of giving up, surrendering herself to the black man's weight and letting him do what he wanted. It was, in all the density of the girl's unwilling flesh, a small warm spasm of real desire, a pang of hunger produced by the heat of close struggle. This was a wrestler's passion which came savagely, suddenly, when the black man rubbed her breasts, squeezed the loose flesh along the girl's side and then rammed his hand between her legs and forced them apart. The spasm grew, paralysed her, a sweet cramp – almost welcome – weakening her will to fight back. It was more than a surrender of will; it was heat, unmistakably sexual, something the girl thought could not occur against her will. But it was happening and, as all the times before, B.J. whimpered, felt the vision seize and shake her. As the black man stroked the girl and slobbered at her neck, disgust rose in B.J.'s throat and weakened her. It was not rancid hatred; it was the wet reality of animal desire mixing with the knowledge of this weakness, for while her mind was made up, her body was not. The outraged mind and undecided body were two separate things: a wisp of will and caution fluttering over a bundle of pawed muscles. It made B.J. ache and the girl sob, 'Don't, please don't.'

'Yes,' whispered the black man. He repeated this over and over, rubbing the word into the girl's ear as he rubbed his hands over her body.

In a pulsing silence made alive and ugly with the twisted face of the girl disappearing under the dark shadow of the man, B.J. fell back, captive to the vision. The black man clapped his hand over the girl's face, hiding her the more and forcing her flat on the seat until her head was caught under the thick arm-rest on the car-door. This made B.J.'s forehead smart; all the girl's useless squirming caused pain and so roused sympathy and pity in B.J. The girl's legs were tangled in the black man's, she tasted bitter acid on his heavy palm and panicked, struggled with her free arm and tried to sit up; but the arm-rest over her forehead prevented her from moving. The black man gripped the side of her shorts; there was a binding tightness at her waist, then the release of this tension on her flesh as the shorts ripped free. They passed over her knees like liquid as the black man freed his legs and pushed the shorts past her ankles.

The man's hand was heavy; it smothered and sickened the girl. When the girl tried to shout, the thick part of the palm sagged into her mouth. The man's other hand fumbled with her legs, a rough fondling of her naked skin, while the hand in her mouth opened her jaws and moved between her teeth. The first pain began in her belly and she bit at the hard palm-flesh, as if at a sour fruit, her saliva running on to the palm and down her chin. Still she bit and moaned, harder and harder, as her head was bumped against the car-door in a brutal rhythm. Her teeth were pressed deeply into the palm. Several minutes later the bumping stopped, the hand slackened. The hand was gone, the girl's mouth empty, running with drool, her body no longer constricted. The girl was motionless.

B.J. drew a deep, deep breath. There was no pain in her body: she was completely exhausted and alone, a cool breeze lapping her legs. She felt weightless and lifted her head dreamily; in half-sleep she looked down at her two white legs, now far apart, like those of a large doll, one flat along the bed, the other raised, bent slightly. Between these, the wall where the girl had sobbed was uncluttered by the shapes that had terrified her. The rag of light was gone.

But something remained, a small figure, shadowy as an incubus, near the bed, at the far edge of the white loop the sprawling legs made.

'Who is it?' B.J. was dizzy; she tried to focus on the figure but could not. It stood, mute and indistinct. B.J. called out again, fearfully, raising herself up on one elbow.

The figure spoke: the voice was soft as the darkness, as if it were being uttered through a curtain of dense cloth.

'What do you want?' B.J.'s voice broke.

The figure glowered, but there was no movement. It was simply a lump, with certain edges that suggested human features. It seemed to crouch in the room like a fly, twitching its mandibles, jerking its head left and right, its whole dark body smeared with filth.

B.J. heard 'No' echoing in her head, but she could not tell if she were thinking it or screaming it. She slid from her bed and ran to the door, pulled at it, all the while her head drumming *No, No, No!* The figure made no move, only stood as B.J. fumbled with the key; its shape had altered and now it seemed to be smiling, gloating with powerfully evil confidence. B.J. dashed into the darkened hallway and out of the house; feeling the strong presence of the thing at her back, she pounded across the garden, swished into the grass to where the slope of the boggy meadow carried her easily down, faster and faster. She heard the rushing of stream-water and ran to it, knowing the water would make her safe. The grass became longer, running was difficult, and then there were bamboo stalks bumping; she pushed the bamboo aside, but they snapped back at her and tore into her flesh. Beyond them were reeds and papyrus that brushed and scraped her face as she fought through them towards the roar of the water. And as each thing touched her – the deep grass, the bamboo stalks, the reeds, the hairy tufts of papyrus – it was as if those black arms pursuing her had reached out to embrace her and, as she pulled away, clawed her.

Her feet sank in the soft bog and sucked as she panted forward; water dribbled through her toes and a peculiar weightlessness came over her – her breath leaving her in a gasp – as she shot downward into water shoulder-deep. Her legs were stuck in mud and went deeper as she thrashed her arms, struggling to float.

B.J. looked up one last time before the mud gave way: she was in churning blackness, being sucked breathlessly down from the black air to the black swamp. The incubus had pursued her, embraced her, engulfed her in sensational black folds. In her ears a riot of liquid voices started, an annoying roar of bubbles that increased in volume as she gulped the poisonous blackness; she swallowed again, and again her mouth was filled with a demon's sour fingers. Her body became stupid with heaviness, like the water around it.

19
Police

Exhausted with worry, Miss Male had gone to bed early on Sunday evening and had been awakened only once in the night: there were sounds from B.J.'s room; a door had clicked open; a busy mumbling and movement was quickly drowned in the hubbub of night noises. Miss Male had listened; she heard locusts scraping tunelessly on broken instruments, bats hurrying through the sky like nimble marks of punctuation and emitting ear-splitting squeals, the frogs and hylas hammering and sawing in the boggy meadow and a steady giggling down where the stream splashed. Miss Male drowsily muttered, 'Good', thinking that B.J. had pulled out of her shock and was now quietly asleep.

On Monday morning the silence in the house startled and sobered Miss Male as the crying had the previous day. She got out of bed and saw that B.J.'s bedroom door was ajar and that B.J. was not in the rumpled bed or anywhere in the room. The room was scattered with dropped clothes and swirls of dirty laundry; it looked as if a struggle had taken place in it – contradictory evidence, for the disorder could have meant that it had been occupied by lovers or enemies. Miss Male hurried to the school but saw no one except – as she crossed the lawn and made her way along the hedge of bougainvillea to the Staff Room – Miss Poole in her car flashing at top speed down the driveway and into the main road, throwing up dust.

Heather arrived at eight and found Miss Male dejectedly searching the buildings, opening this door, peeking in that window. Heather said she knew nothing; she had no idea where B.J. could have gone and had heard nothing strange in the night. She said that she had spent the evening writing letters; something, she added, as if revealing the substance of a dark secret, she had not done in a very long while. Miss Male looked puzzled and Heather added, 'They were letters to old girlfriends – women always reply, that's why I think twice about writing to them. But that's how bad things are.' Heather put her lips together softly, thoughtfully, then said, 'As if there aren't enough women here. It's a bloody free-for-all, this bitchery.'

In Miss Poole's absence, Heather agreed to conduct the girls' morning prayers which, that week, was a series of veiled demands for God to help them pass their end-of-term exams. The girls were pathetically pious; several in the back of the room keened in piercing misery like pilgrims at a shrine. All knelt and with heads bent intoned the wooden prayer, 'Guide my hand and heart and head, O Lord, in this decisive moment. Make me steadfast and strong ... etc.' With gusto, as if it were a magical incantation, they ended the morning prayers with all the stanzas of 'Land of Hope and Glory'. Heather conducted the singing with a knitting needle and hoped desperately that Miss Poole would turn up in time to hear the song.

Milky, heavily sugared coffee was served at ten in the Staff Room, but only Miss Male and Heather were there to drink it. While they sat thoughtfully stirring the tinkling cups, the door swung open abruptly. Miss Male dropped her spoon; Heather held her coffee in her mouth and could not swallow it. But it was not B.J. It was Miss Verjee looking for the netball. She said she had not seen B.J. for nearly a week.

When Miss Verjee left, Heather imitated her saying, 'I hev not zeen her for nearly a veek.'

'I'm going to tell the police,' said Miss Male. She cradled her coffee cup in two hands near her face, like a crystal ball.

'Whatever for?'

'It's the proper drill, isn't it? You can never –'

Heather was about to say 'rubbish', but she noticed that there were tears forming in Miss Male's eyes. She said, 'If it'll make you feel better, by all means go to the police and report it. Cheer up, Pam, everything's going to be all right. Take my car if you want.'

'I think you'd better keep it here. If B.J. turns up you might have to take her to the hospital.'

'What did you say?' Heather looked at Miss Male as if at a lunatic.

'To the hospital. I know this is silly, but I think something is terribly wrong. Something terrible's happened to B.J., I'm sure of it.'

'You're jumping to conclusions,' said Heather.

'I wouldn't say that. I always think about your story, the one about the woman who was strangled near here. It was so horrible –'

'Pam, I'm afraid I exaggerated that one a bit,' said Heather sheepishly. 'But Miss Poole made me so bloody angry –'

'You mean it didn't happen?' Miss Male started to smile.

'Not here – that is, not in East Africa. I think it happened in ... was it Nigeria? One of those countries. I read about it in the *News of the World*.'

'Then you lied.'

'I suppose I did then, didn't I? But that's rather a bald way of putting it.' Heather tried to laugh. 'Anyway, take my car and for goodness sake stop worrying about B.J.'

Miss Male closed her eyes and sighed; there was a smile of relief on her lips. 'I feel much better,' she said. She smiled at Heather, then lifted her arm, squeezed her watch and said, 'It's after ten. I'd better run. I won't have any trouble getting a lift.'

On the main road, Miss Male inhaled the fragrance of the flowering trees and stretched the worry out of her arms. A few minutes later, a Landrover approached on the main road; it rattled to a halt next to her. A plastic side window was slid back. An African policeman stuck his head out.

'You are a teacher here?' The African's tongue was pure pink, a lovely bubble-gum colour, with white chiclets of teeth pressing it lightly.

'Yes, I am,' said Miss Male. 'I'm on my way to the police station, as a matter of fact. I wonder if you'd –'

'Get in, please.'

'You see,' said Miss Male in the back seat, 'I'm rather worried about my friend.' The engine of the Landrover whined; Miss Male's seat jogged up and down. 'She seems to have been away all night.'

The African twisted his neck so that he was watching the road with one eye and shouting to Miss Male in the back with part of his face. 'I served in Burma Campaign in King's African Rifles. British liked me. Got ribbons, too, nice ones, man. Rangoon, Bombay, Aden, even India, myself I've been there. Give me cigarette.'

20

Confidential

'It's a pity,' Wilbur said, scraping his chair up to the desk and tugging a stack of fat files towards him. 'We education officers don't see the schools as much as we would like. But I'm sure you realize that we're very busy with one thing and another.'

'Yes, yes, of course,' said Miss Poole. She had been waiting in the office since eight, the official opening time of government offices; it was now past ten and already breathlessly hot. It would be a scorching day; Miss Poole did not like to think of what the heat would do to her tar patches on the roof tiles. The last hot spell had caused many of them to bubble and drip through to the desks.

Rumpled, though with dignity, Miss Poole stood in Wilbur's office clutching an old handbag of flaking snakeskin; she was stiff, but this was not nervousness so much as good posture. Her raised chin, head tilted back, revealed a considerable amount of her scrawny neck. She wore sunglasses very similar to Rose's and a wide straw hat with a faded pink ribbon band, the sort that might have been worn at a garden fête twenty years ago. Her long shapeless shoulder-padded dress was stained darkly at the armpits with perspiration. She was at attention. She watched Wilbur bury his face in his handkerchief and then wipe the sweat-slime that glistened on his neck.

'Please sit down. I'm sorry I wasn't here when you arrived. Monday morning.' Wilbur chuckled in embarrassment. 'It's the one day when everyone is late for work.'

Ordinarily Miss Poole would have replied, 'Not *quite* everyone,' but she had other things on her mind, and in fact was surprised that Wilbur had appeared at all. She had feared that she would have to tell her story to a junior officer. She sat stiffly on the edge of the wicker chair, her back straight. She placed the handbag on her lap and folded her hands over it tightly. 'I understand,' she said.

'Now what can I do for you?' Wilbur said pleasantly. He opened and shut one of the files, subtly fanning himself.

'It's rather urgent,' Miss Poole began uncertainly. 'I've come on a very urgent matter. It's one of the members of my staff. I know it's a bit irregular of me not to have brought her along, but I want you to understand that it's a rather delicate situation. I wanted to have your strictest confidence.'

Wilbur nodded approvingly. Humming in assent through his nose, he walked to the open door, peered outside, told the messenger to buzz off, and shut the door. The air in the room stirred when the door slammed, then was still, thick and hot with dusty office-odours. Wilbur returned to his chair behind the desk, leaned towards Miss Poole and said, 'Go on.'

'I hardly know where to begin,' said Miss Poole. She had planned to start by telling about the first dinner party and Heather's blasphemous remark, but instead, and without thinking, she told how the person in question (which was how she referred to Heather) showed up at the school and turned her vicious dog on a defenceless little cat. She described how the cat had been savaged and then went on to the blasphemy. Wilbur smiled; Miss Poole did not pause. She told him of the dinners, of the coffee that was poured on her foot and the smoke puffed into her face in the dark, the collapsing chairs, the nuisance Jacko made of himself, the wilful destruction of the science laboratory and the burning of the library annexe. Using one of the Form Four girls as a typical example, she described how in one term the girl's grades had worsened, how she had grown insolent and unmanageable and, were the situation to continue, would most probably end up on the streets. The other teachers, Miss Poole said, had been most pleasant, but even they were becoming strangely unruly. The person in question was against having exams and said the most horrible things about the school, the girls and the country in general. She was, not to put too fine a point on it, dangerous, and would have to go.

'Yes, that does sound very serious to me,' said Wilbur. 'But I'm sure you know that it's not easy to get transfers for people that have trouble adjusting.'

'She wants to be Headmistress, can you imagine such a thing? She's been trying her best, by lying and gossip, to discredit me. I believe she would use physical violence to get what she wants.' Miss Poole craned towards Wilbur and added, 'I am sure of that. She would do anything, anything at all.'

'But transfers –'

'I am suggesting that she be forced to resign,' Miss Poole interrupted, 'not transferred. She should leave the teaching profession completely and the Ministry should recommend her deportation as soon as possible. She is simply not fit to go on.'

Wilbur shook his head. 'I have the power to do this – I could do it today if I wanted to – but in my years in this Ministry I haven't known anyone that was forced to resign and then deported. We usually send these sticky cases to the bush and, well,' Wilbur cackled, '*this* is the bush!'

'I haven't told you everything,' Miss Poole said curtly.

'Please do,' Wilbur said. He now took out a pencil and

a large piece of lined foolscap. He poised his pencil over the paper and looked across his desk at Miss Poole.

'In a girls' school,' Miss Poole began in her preaching tone, 'there is one thing we must always insist upon. That is morality. We try to teach our girls the highest standards of behaviour, and we cannot do this, we can never possibly do this,' Miss Poole said in churchy repetition, 'unless we practise this behaviour ourselves. If one girl notices that we are slackening, she will take advantage of it, and others will follow.' She clenched her bag tightly; translucent scales danced from the snakeskin. She continued: 'We teach by example. If our example is not of the very highest, discipline breaks down and there is chaos, moral and spiritual chaos. Morality to me, sir, means much more than good manners.'

'What exactly did this woman do?' asked Wilbur impatiently.

'I will come to the point. This is not simply a woman blotting her copybook. This is a clear-cut case of deliberate immorality.'

'How do you know she's immoral?'

'She has men spending the night with her,' Miss Poole said quickly, as if she were emptying her mouth of something vile. 'This is the sort of thing we cannot tolerate.'

'It's hard to prove these things. You need witnesses, people have to sign things and swear –'

'I have witnesses.'

'Well,' Wilbur fished for a question, 'maybe it was her boyfriend.'

'Boyfriends are one thing. I have often had the gentlemen friends of my staff members to tea. I encourage that. I enjoy meeting them and always had Julius make fresh cheese straws for them. But this is something else entirely. This is immorality.'

'I wish you would be more specific.'

'I shall. On Saturday last, a man was found in the house of the person in question. The man was dead drunk and reeking of alcohol, sleeping on her bedroom floor in a state of undress.'

'Sleeping on the floor you say?' Wilbur began doodling softly on the sheet of paper.

'On the floor. He was seen by my most trusted employee. I might add, with all respect, that he was an African.'

Wilbur dug the point of the pencil down through the paper and anchored it to the blotter. He twirled it and said, 'Yes, hm, I think I am in the picture now. Have you any idea who this . . . African is?'

'None whatever,' Miss Poole said promptly. 'But I am sure he can be found. People talk. I might add that I consider *him* just as guilty as the person in question. I was hoping you might ask about – there are no secrets here. It shouldn't be hard to find out who the man is.'

'You don't have any idea who it might be?'

'I haven't a clue.'

'I'll do what I can,' said Wilbur carefully. 'Now if you give me the teacher's name I'll get straight to work on this case.'

Miss Poole said the name in her usual way, pronouncing it again like the name of the furry ichneumon.

Before Wilbur could react, there was a knock at the door which jerked the muscles in his face. He blinked and worked his mouth. Miss Poole turned her head towards the door and watched it.

'One moment!' Wilbur shouted.

The rapping continued, reminding Miss Poole of her old terror: as soon as a door closed in East Africa, someone was banging on it to be opened. Wilbur cursed and shoved his creaking chair back in anger, but by the time he had risen the door was open: coolness entered the room, the air stirred. Two huge policemen stood there, in sharply creased shorts, puttees and cork helmets. They saluted Wilbur, bowed to Miss Poole, and one spoke in a slushy vernacular that was not Swahili. Miss Poole sat with her back to the men and did not pay attention until, near the end of the gabbled monologue, she heard a strangled cluster of consonants, 'Fitch', and then a word she had once heard from Rose, 'Wangi'. The second was a common name in those parts, but the first she knew belonged to only one man.

21

Faces at the Window

There were about thirty Africans at the police station, some milling around in the sun, others watching silently from under the shady flame trees at the side. They gathered around the Landrover when it swerved up to the veranda. The engine shuddered off; as Miss Male climbed out, the Africans pressed around her, staring slack-mouthed with empty inquiring faces, like deprived tourists. The policemen pushed the crowd aside roughly and let Miss Male pass.

Inside the main door, sitting near a policeman on a wooden bench, was Fitch. Seeing Miss Male on the veranda, he scrambled to his feet. He was haggard, the stubble on his face soaked with bristly sweat-droplets; he wore only an undershirt and trousers; there were torn sandals on his dusty, sockless feet; his hairy toes protruded. The undershirt was stained and damp, the trousers out at the knees. He sneezed shamelessly into Miss Male's face, then blew his nose into his fingers.

'Been up since four,' he said. 'Froze my flipping arse at four and now I'm sweating. Fooking big *shauri* with your friend.' He looked again at Miss Male and then shook his head. 'But *you're* not the one.'

'This way,' the policeman said. He walked into the building.

'I hope I haven't caused you any trouble,' Fitch said. 'You're not the one I had in mind, but all the same I'm glad to see you. They've been asking me a right lot of questions. My boys found the body on their way to work. They came and got me out of bed. She was undressed, mostly. They didn't want anyone to think they had anything to do with it. Thought I'd explain for them. Christ!' Fitch wiped his mouth on his hairy forearm. 'The way I see it, the body must have floated a fair distance – pretty strong current in that stream. And she might have bloated up, you see. Well, I took one look at her and says to myself, I *know* her, she was with the fat bloke on Friday night she was, and the little chap from the Electricity Board and ... bloody hell, when I reported it they started a great argy-bargy about who was she and when did I see her before ...'

The policeman waved them forward and continued walking. Miss Male speeded up; Fitch followed behind, still explaining.

'... I couldn't lie. I got my business to think of. They could finish me, *kabisa* – take my licence away. I told them everything I knew. Saw her just last Friday, I says. She's a Yank, told me so herself. They called the Peace Corps chaps in Nairobi. They're on their way here now, flying in their own plane. Christ, there's no end to the money they got. I couldn't tell them anything except there was another *mzungu* along with her; from the school, I says. But I didn't know I'd get *you* mixed up in this, expected they'd get the other one, the noisy one that wears all the make-up on her face –'

'Heather,' said Miss Male softly, to show Fitch that she had been listening.

'That's the one. She'd know something about this, wouldn't she? They was friends, wasn't they? I hope you can straighten this thing out. These bleeding sods won't let me go home until someone identifies the body. I don't know her name, you see, though she told me once. I'm bloody glad you're here. Maybe I can go now. Hope I haven't caused you any trouble. Thought you was the other one, the noisy one.'

They were now outside a large door at the far end of the corridor. The policeman took a key-ring and inserted a jangling key in the lock. It was medieval; the black man in the gloomy corridor, the long antique key, the thick scarred planks of the door. He pushed the heavy door in; it squeaked on rusty hinges. The dark room was cool and smelled of swamp water.

Miss Male had dreaded the moment. When the policeman flicked on the overhead light and lifted the blanket, it occurred to her that since early in the morning, when she awoke, she had seen a dozen blankets being lifted on a dozen slabs in her mind. And each had revealed exactly what she now saw before her: a damp face, bloodless and going blue, speckled with bits of petal and broken green leaf; the hair, thick, water-darkened, was spread on the table behind the head, exposing a broad chalky forehead. B.J. could not have been mistaken for a sleeper; she was rigid and dead, her eyes were staring up, her lips, tinged with blue, were open in a fishy O of stupefaction.

'Yes,' said Miss Male. She tried to say more, but could only utter gulps; she put her hands to her face and sobbed uncontrollably.

Stamping, Wilbur appeared at the door looking agitated. He called to Miss Male, 'Is that your friend, the American?' He pointed towards the corpse.

Miss Male did not answer; she walked to the musty wall, rested her forehead against it and wept, ignoring Wilbur.

'That's the Yank there,' said Fitch, tossing his head. 'And it's a right bloody shame, to my way of thinking.'

'Come here, Fitch,' said Wilbur urgently. 'I want to talk to you.'

Miss Male had been shown to a side-room by one of the policemen. The room was damp, with buntings of dirt-flecked cobwebs on the ceiling boards. On one wall, poked on a bent nail, was a picture of the Royal Family standing in a row on a lawn that had once showed green. Miss Male sat hunched over a blackened table with her fists against her eyes. She looked up and saw that she was in near-darkness: there were African faces at the window, peering at her through the dirty glass and thick bars, blocking the sunlight. The faces saddened and enraged her; she shivered in the coolness of the shaded room and wept again. She saw B.J. in her fists, frozen in many laughing poses, as if she were flipping through a pack of her snapshots. Miss Male was weary; it seemed days since she had woken up and sensed the silence, saw the swirls of clothes in the room and B.J.'s empty bed. In her belly she felt an emptiness, a forlorn hunger that nothing could satisfy. She whimpered. There were no more tears. Her arms were streaked where her tears had run through dust and dried.

The door opened; a man stood in the doorway. He was tall, pink, and wore a new bush shirt, shorts and alpine boots; his hair was burned blonde. He hesitated, almost drew back, when Miss Male faced him. Her cheeks were lined, pale with shock. Her eyes puffed, red-rimmed; her nose was raw from being blown.

'The sergeant said you were here,' the man said uneasily. 'Sorry for busting in on you like this.'

Miss Male tried to speak, but found she could only mumble; she was frightened to hear her weak voice. She shrugged sadly and began again to cry.

'I know how you feel.' The man nodded. 'She was a great kid.'

New tears had started down Miss Male's cheeks where other tears had left dry trails. She dabbed at her eyes and pressed her lips together to prevent a repetition of her half-human mumbling. The man took her hand and she was comforted; the man was also trembling.

The man said that his name was Chuck and that he was on the Peace Corps staff. He had been sent to escort the body to Nairobi. The trouble was that the body could not be moved until a post-mortem was done on it, to determine the cause of death. A doctor was on his way in a van. As soon as the doctor said it was okay they would leave by road.

Miss Male found her voice. 'Take me with you, please. I want to go home. I can get my plane fare from the British Council.'

'Sure,' said Chuck, smiling. 'I'll take you. There's always room for one more.' He untwisted his grin; his face fell. 'Sorry. That didn't sound right.'

Miss Male had not heard. The thought of going re-laxed her; tension left her body, deserting the sadness that stayed.

'Say, you don't look too hot.'

'I feel unwell. This has all been a great strain.'

'I'll bet,' said Chuck. 'It's a rotten thing to happen. Can I give you a lift back to your school?'

'I'd rather not see it just yet. I don't think I'm ... ready.' Miss Male laughed weakly, then her face crumpled; she seemed on the point of tears again.

'Look,' said Chuck earnestly, 'I'm supposed to be stay-ing up the road at a place called the Horse and Hunter. Why don't you come along with me and have lunch? I'll give you a ride back to your school later this afternoon.

I'd be much obliged if you came. I guess I need company as much as you do.'

Miss Male rose; Chuck took her arm. They were at the door when the faces at the window disappeared; the room filled with light.

On the way to the Horse and Hunter Chuck tried to make conversation. He said the countryside was the prettiest he had ever laid eyes on, so green. There were sunbirds on the trees near the police station; they had lovely curved beaks, but made an awful racket. Still, it was a beautiful country.

'I used to think that,' said Miss Male to the window. Africa was green, even lush, but lushness made death possible. B.J. had died in a clutter of flowers; there were petals on her dead face.

'Any idea who did it?' Chuck did not take his eyes off the road.

Miss Male did not answer.

Fitch smelled trouble when he saw the stranger arrive with Miss Male. He knew he was being spied on and, after all Wilbur had said to him, regretted having reported the incident to the police. He vowed he would say nothing more. In silence he showed Chuck to the thatch-roofed hut. He got drinks – a beer for Chuck, an orange squash for Miss Male – then ducked behind the bar, downed a double whisky and fled for the day.

On the veranda Chuck whispered that Fitch looked like a real character. 'Right out of Graham Greene,' he said.

A waiter announced lunch.

Throughout lunch Miss Male maintained silence. She ate slowly, thoughtfully cutting and spearing meat and potatoes. A whole conversation came to her, but she felt too shy to begin. Americans always asked for definitions, explanations, and sometimes they misunderstood. She had wanted to ask Chuck why he was in Africa. She no longer knew why she had come.

Over dessert, Chuck said, as if reading her thoughts, 'Africa. I used to think –' He stopped spooning his custard and stared. His face had the pained incomprehension of someone who had just been robbed.

Late in the afternoon Chuck drove Miss Male back to the school compound. He dropped her at the driveway and said he'd see her in the morning. As Miss Male walked up the driveway she noticed there were no girls on the playing field, although it was past four. There seemed to be great activity over at the dorms, a bustle of girls sweeping, stacking boxes and suitcases, flapping and folding sheets and blankets on the grass.

Heather was standing in the driveway near Miss Poole's signboard. She did not speak until Miss Male started towards Miss Poole's house.

'She's gone,' Heather said. 'They took her away.'

Miss Male turned and looked closely at Heather. 'Miss Poole?'

'Gone,' Heather said simply. She wore no make-up and looked different, old; her lips were narrow and dry, her face cross-hatched with thin lines that powder had always covered. Without either eyebrows or lashes, her eyes – her whole face – was empty and expressionless, as Miss Poole's had been for most of the time Miss Male had known her. Her hair was discoloured and grey at the roots; one dry strand draped the side of her face.

'The police came for her with the education officer,' Heather said in the voice of a sleepwalker. She spoke without alarm, but as she did, Miss Male formed vivid pictures in her mind of what Heather described: the police Landrover arriving at noon and stopping at Miss Poole's front door, the policeman leaping out and ordering the old lady to get into the vehicle. Bewildered, Miss Poole had hesitated and gone stiff in her chair. She had to be dragged out, like a small girl being yanked off a playground by rough servants. She had stumbled on the steps, her legs had given way. One of the policemen thought she was trying to escape and in panic smacked her across the face with his riding crop.

'It was ghastly,' Heather droned, 'ghastly. They pushed her into the front seat. She went all pale and began to shake. She looked straight ahead through the windscreen and I knew she hated me. I knew it. I wanted to say, "I didn't do this to you. I don't like you –"' Heather's voice began to implore an invisible figure on the grass. '"I never liked you, but I'd never do this to you, not this. It was all fair until this, and I didn't do it."'

After a pause, during which the insects and frogs down at the stream and the swaying leaves on the flame-tree boughs near the playing field combined in the usual nightfall crackle and hush, a reminder of the drooping cables of wild vines that lay just beyond the compound, Miss Male said, 'You've heard about B.J.?'

'On the bush telegraph. One of the girls told me, after you'd gone. It's monstrous. Everything's gone wrong. They think Miss Poole had something to do with it. Indirectly, of course. They're hoping to hush it up by deporting her.'

Miss Male shook her head. She turned and looked across the empty playing field. 'How are the girls taking it?'

'I told them to pack up. Miss Verjee resigned when she heard about B.J. She thought it was an uprising. Terrorists, you know. I tried to explain, but she wouldn't listen. She was scared out of her wits. She must be in

Nairobi by now, but she's all right, isn't she, getting married.' Heather lit a cigarette. 'The girls leave tomorrow on the school lorry. There won't be any exams.'

'I'm leaving,' said Miss Male without feeling. 'I'm going back to England.'

'That's definite?'

Miss Male nodded.

'You'd better put it in writing. Address the letter to me. After they took Miss Poole away, Wilbur made me Headmistress.'

22

The Last Girl

Miss Male was packing when Heather came over on Tuesday morning. At first Heather said nothing. She sat in a chair smoking, kicking a crossed leg up and down nervously. Miss Male went on with her packing; she had had a sleepless night and was doing a bad job of folding the curtains, sorting a vast accumulation of files and notes, and wrapping the crockery in newspapers. She worked haphazardly, at one thing, then another, when the disorder caught her eye; she stepped from the pile of folders to the bundle of unfolded cloth. A dish broke, she cursed under her breath. All the things she stuffed in a large black trunk which, on the front, gave her name, the school's address and the freight instruction *via Mombasa*. The name of the port made Heather think of her trip out, the horror stories in the ship's bar, the anxious retching in her cabin, the man who got off at Aden. It had happened long ago and, it seemed, to another woman.

'The girls have just left,' Heather said. 'There were a few complaints about the seating arrangements, but they'll sort themselves out.'

Miss Male looked up from a tangle of twine and brown paper. 'Sorry I didn't get a chance to say good-bye. But there's so much to pack. I'm doing B.J.'s as well. She had masses of things, poor dear.'

'Americans,' Heather said. 'I knew one who brought a year's supply of toilet rolls with him. Can you imagine?'

Miss Male turned away.

'Can I give you a hand?'

'Thanks no,' said Miss Male softly. 'I'm nearly done, thank goodness. I've just got to find space for these curios.' She stood surrounded by drums, an oval red-painted shield, a little spear, a pair of carved kudu. In her hand was a small ebony figurine, a naked crouching man with exaggerated features. She dropped it in a box which bore B.J.'s name.

'That's an interesting walking-stick,' said Heather. She pointed to the gnarled stick with the head and foot of a monkey that the old man had given to B.J.

'It was B.J.'s,' said Miss Male. 'Take it, if you'd like. I'm sure she would have given it to you. She was very generous, you know.'

Heather received the stick gladly. She would treasure it; like many plain things she owned, it had a story. Heather said, 'She was Jewish. I don't know what made me think of that.'

'Yes. She told me. She didn't take it too seriously, though. She wasn't a Golders Green type.'

'Her family must be heartbroken. Did anyone remember to send them a telegram?'

'The Peace Corps took care of that. I'm going to write to her father when I get to England. I think he'd be glad.'

'Yes,' said Heather, 'he'd like that.' She looked around the room, then said, 'Please sit down, Pam. There's just the two of us left. I never really knew you very well. I wish I had done. I think we could have been good friends, age differences aside. But you must know all about me –'

Miss Male, who had closed the trunk and seated herself on it, started to rise, protesting. She was silenced by Heather.

'No. Don't be polite. It's common knowledge, my whoring around. But I'm not bad, really I'm not. I used to think it was this place; of course, it's not. Women are – the word is *promiscuous*, I think – because sex is such a bloody let-down. You always think there's going to be more to it, you think you're missing out on something and so you – I suppose I should say *I* – keep trying. That's why women deep down trust the great greasy lovers and let themselves get seduced. They think it's going to be different. Only it's always the same. By the time you've done it twice you're promiscuous and you say what the hell, you don't have anything to lose.'

Heather lit another cigarette and, puffing smoke, said, 'I'll tell you a story. I'm sure you've heard it, but not the way it really happened. There's not much point in going over it again, but I want at least one person to know the truth.'

She told the story plainly; she wanted to be believed, without pity, only with the understanding that she was telling it the way it happened. She had gone out with Colin and liked him. He said all the things she too believed. They enjoyed a mutual vulgar mockery that appeared at times to be consuming their friendship. She tested him by saying she disagreed with him. He did not care. He came after her and she continued to see him and sleep with him. He loathed his wife and even suspected that one of his two children was not really his, though he had no proof. One Easter he took Heather to the Coast. And then he was rude to her, insulting, only once, but that was enough and she knew it was over with him. The month they quarrelled her periods stopped. She had been off-schedule before, but this time not even hormone pills would start a flow. There could only be one explanation: she was pregnant and Colin was the father. She was surprised by her happiness at the prospect of motherhood. Colin refused to see her. She told her friends. The word got round to Colin's wife and there was a visit from the Headmistress of Mainwaring, who was escorted by a chaplain. They explained that as an unmarried mother-to-be she would have to resign and compensate the Government. But the pregnancy had to be verified. She was sent to the government doctor; by then she had gained weight, her belly had swollen noticeably and she was having morning sickness. The doctor ordered an X-ray and this showed a small knob in the uterus, but not a foetus. There were vaginal discharges. An operation was performed and a uterine cyst, a ball of tissue the size of a strawberry, was removed. She could not face her friends and did not dare to talk to Colin. Also she could not be forced to resign. But Colin's wife was circulating stories about her and these she found unbearable. She went to Colin's house to explain. There was a scene. The police were called and Heather arrested for disturbing the peace. Colin's wife was threatening divorce. Heather was transferred.

'It was all nasty,' Heather said. 'There were bad jokes, anonymous letters saying "What got into you?" The rumours were much worse. I thought it might do me some good to come here. Obviously, it hasn't. But, you know, I've never spoken to anyone like this before. I know I have a long life ahead of me – if you know the truth, I can face things much more easily. I couldn't sleep last night because I knew I was going to tell you all this.'

Miss Male was moved by the story, by the frank way Heather told it, as if she were asking for absolution. The version Miss Male had heard had been much milder than Heather's truthful account. 'Why don't you go back to England?' Miss Male asked. 'At least you belong there.'

'I don't think I could stick England now. Besides, there

are such a lot of wogs there. They're coming in by the thousands.'

'What were you doing before you came out here?'

'I was ...' Heather saw a little corner of a shop; there were clothes-racks and large ugly women in old hats picked at dress-sleeves; a shop-assistant with a pencil in her hair, wearing a smock with a little round badge bearing the store's insignia inquired about fabrics on a stained intercom. 'I was in women's fashions,' Heather said. 'I don't have to worry about a job, really. My father has pots of money.'

'Then you don't have any problems, do you?' said Miss Male. But she only said it to calm Heather; Miss Male (Cheltenham, St Anne's, heiress to a brewery) was certain she was lying. Heather, she guessed, was lower-middle and it was a pity, for the people in the lower-middle classes lived long and never had money. 'Weren't you talking about going to the Coast?'

'Oh, that's out now. It's funny. I feel like a hag. As if I've just let go of all my sex. I don't have any now. When I heard B.J. was dead I got scared; then they roughed up Miss Poole. My sex all leaked out. I don't have any instincts any more. I'm an old woman –'

'Don't be silly,' said Miss Male. 'I'll bet you have a lot of friends.'

Heather lowered her voice. 'I used to know a very kind man in Croydon, a funny old thing, kind of sexy and not-sexy at the same time. I don't know why I'm telling you all this. I sometimes wonder where he is. I'd like to find him, or someone like him. Not to have any children, I'm probably beyond that. But just someone who's kind, to live with, go for walks –'

She did look years older. And as she looked at her, Miss Male was saddened by all that had happened. For six months Miss Male had been happy; in one fearful weekend she had seen sadness, cruelty and death close up, and now she knew she could never be happy again. She had once envied Heather; Heather had seemed tough, gay, with a looseness about her mouth and a decisiveness about saying 'rubbish' that only very free women have. That was gone now. Heather was old, her face was lined, her mouth drawn tight.

In that moment Miss Male wanted to ask, 'Who did it?' as Chuck had asked. But B.J. was dead, it was over, and finding the culprit did not matter. There were many culprits in Africa; and there could be no justice because B.J. had been among strangers and had no business there. There were risks in coming to Africa; Miss Male had taken them; she knew she could expect nothing better than the dead girl in the morgue, the terrorized old lady, the chainsmoker in her parlour. Exiles, they had elected to live alone as girls, unmarried among bananas. It was cruel to think, but they had asked for it.

Chuck came shortly afterwards. He insisted on packing the things in the back of the van while Heather and Miss Male shared a Coke on the grass. Chuck had not wanted them to see the coffin; it was an ugly thing, just a box; an American deserved better.

'I'll write you a letter,' said Miss Male when she was in the van.

'Don't send it to *this* address,' Heather laughed. She waved good-bye with the walking-stick Miss Male had given her.

Heather remained staring until the red dust raised by the van sifted slowly down through the windless air to the road. The school compound was deserted and empty, looked to Heather less like a school than it ever had. It was a garden, once formal, now overgrown with lush green, pulpous fruit, heavy blossoms; the buildings were scarcely visible without the girls running around them. Some sleek green birds shot from tree to bush, gave a short whistle, then flew on. The weavers in their bunched nests in the bamboos near the driveway twittered crazily, a sound Heather heard for the first time, though they had been there a long while. It was noon, the sun blasted everywhere.

The police would come in the afternoon. In spite of Wilbur's bribe in promoting her, she had sent a note to the police. Practising her new thoughtfulness, she had kept this fact from Miss Male; she did not want Miss Male involved as a witness in a court case. Heather wanted to be alone in testifying; she would tell everything, every last detail of the Friday night and all Miss Male had related. Some people came to Africa and wrote books about their experiences; she would have the witness stand, a court packed with listeners, a stenographer noting it all down for the newspapers. Wilbur's feeble bribe angered her. '*She's* the cause of all this,' Wilbur had said when Miss Poole was still in the Landrover. 'This is the end of it, isn't it? Now you can run the school right. She was a settler, you know.' Proof of connivance (and this she longed to tell), Wilbur had winked. He would get what he deserved, as, cruelly, she always had. Heather spat air.

Before she went into her house Heather walked around the school grounds to make sure the dorms were locked, the classrooms and office in order. All the buildings were neat, with a one-day accumulation of powdery wood-dust which had filtered down from the ants and bore-beetles in their rafter holes. She bent to blow a smear of it from a desk when she heard a faint sound, a soft shuffle, like something being dragged across the gritty cement of the veranda.

'Is there anyone here?' Her voice sounded silly to her, echoing in the empty classroom. It died out and then the hot room trilled with insects. She felt embarrassed to have called out to no one. It might have been Rufus who, having disappeared the night of B.J.'s death, had not come back. Trudging pointlessly through bush, following endless taunting odours, he ate fieldmice; he was often away for days, and then he would show up almost apologetic, with a cut paw, burrs and seeds clinging to his knotted coat, like an errant husband.

There was little food in the pantry. Heather found a tomato with crow's feet, part of a crumpled envelope of dried Swiss soup, a half-box of biscuits which had gone soft, and two heavily freckled bananas. In a fit of stubborn melancholy she wished that Jacko was still with her. He would have made something of the pitiful fragments and served it on a starched white tablecloth; there would be fresh scones for tea. But he had never come back.

She ate off the sideboard, standing up, to save carrying the dishes to the sink. When she had finished she rinsed the pan and dropped the spattered soup-bowl, the spoon and knife into it to wash-up later. Leaving the kitchen, she faced the full sun streaming into the living-room and went faint in the heat; she had to touch the wall for balance: the room swam with tropical light, white and dizzying. The moment passed. She drew the blinds on all the windows, locked the doors and went to her bedroom to lie down. Her VW was in the driveway; the police were not cretins, they would see it and knock.

She stirred slightly when the lock clicked in the kitchen door, but rolled over and, as always, grasped the spongey pillow around her ears. A rhinoceros beetle droned outside, strafing and bouncing off a window-pane where it saw the garden reflected. Heather snored, asleep; she heard nothing.

The house was dark, but Rose did not need light to see where she was going; she knew the arrangement of rooms. All staff houses were built to one blueprint by government order. Making a scraping sound with her coarse feet dragging on the hard floor, Rose moved into the hallway and paused before the bedroom door. The air of the darkened house on her burned skin gave her relief; she breathed the coolness. In her hand was a carving knife; the cutting edge was jagged, saw-toothed; the point, seldom used, was needle-sharp. She tested it with her finger and, in her own darkness, was not even aware that she drew blood.

The bedroom door opened easily, noiselessly, only the bunch of keys making a clink as Rose slipped them into her apron pocket. Heather lay on the narrow bed with her back to the door. Rose leaned forward and peered, but saw only blocks of grey fuzz. The straining to see made her eyes itch; she removed the dark glasses, put them on the floor, and the room lightened, the rounded bulk of the sleeping woman swam in and out of focus. Rose shuffled closer, scraping left foot, right foot, left foot, until she was near the bed. Gripping the moist wooden handle of the knife in her two bruised hands, she raised it over Heather's neck, just below the thin jaw-bone. Heather opened her eyes when she heard Rose shriek, but by then the knife was less than an inch from her throat, Rose was stabbing down.

The first stroke glanced off Heather's neck; the second ripped a flap of skin, dug through ribbons of muscle and struck bone. Rose stabbed again, a morlock mewing over Heather's neck, and continued to stab until she weakened. The hard thrusts became a savage sawing with the jagged blade. She stopped when Heather arched her back. Realizing that she could not see or gulp air, Heather sobbed a spout of blood. Her face twisted; she tried to complain; as she sank back into the bed, her head lolled heavily to the side, sticky with blood.

Rose is off, the last girl. She drops the knife and, crunching her glasses, stumbles out of the house. She crosses Heather's garden, trampling the violets, barging into the fat-limbed frangipani. Raggedly, falling forwards, she hurries across the main lawn (bordered by bougain-villea trimmed square) to the playing field (with its high fence of flame trees), knees pumping wildly, skirts flying, splay-mouthed. And then, for no reason at all, she stops running and simply stands as if discovering she is trapped, alone on the broad green field, a white mottled dwarf, one arm across her stricken eyes against the agony of the afternoon sun.

FOR THE BEST IN PAPERBACKS, LOOK FOR THE 🐧

In every corner of the world, on every subject under the sun, Penguin represents quality and variety – the very best in publishing today.

For complete information about books available from Penguin – including Pelicans, Puffins, Peregrines and Penguin Classics – and how to order them, write to us at the appropriate address below. Please note that for copyright reasons the selection of books varies from country to country.

In the United Kingdom: Please write to *Dept E.P., Penguin Books Ltd, Harmondsworth, Middlesex, UB7 0DA*

In the United States: Please write to *Dept BA, Penguin, 299 Murray Hill Parkway, East Rutherford, New Jersey 07073*

In Canada: Please write to *Penguin Books Canada Ltd, 2801 John Street, Markham, Ontario L3R 1B4*

In Australia: Please write to the *Marketing Department, Penguin Books Australia Ltd, P.O. Box 257, Ringwood, Victoria 3134*

In New Zealand: Please write to the *Marketing Department, Penguin Books (NZ) Ltd, Private Bag, Takapuna, Auckland 9*

In India: Please write to *Penguin Overseas Ltd, 706 Eros Apartments, 56 Nehru Place, New Delhi, 110019*

In Holland: Please write to *Penguin Books Nederland B.V., Postbus 195, NL–1380AD Weesp, Netherlands*

In Germany: Please write to *Penguin Books Ltd, Friedrichstrasse 10–12, D–6000 Frankfurt Main 1, Federal Republic of Germany*

In Spain: Please write to *Longman Penguin España, Calle San Nicolas 15, E–28013 Madrid, Spain*

In France: Please write to *Penguin Books Ltd, 39 Rue de Montmorency, F-75003, Paris, France*

In Japan: Please write to *Longman Penguin Japan Co Ltd, Yamaguchi Building, 2–12–9 Kanda Jimbocho, Chiyoda-Ku, Tokyo 101, Japan*

The Mosquito Coast

Allie Fox was going to recreate the world. Abominating the cops, crooks, scavengers and funny bunnies of the twentieth century, he abandons civilization and takes the family to live in the Honduran jungle. There his tortured, quixotic genius keeps them alive, his hoarse tirades harrying them through a diseased and dirty Eden towards unimaginable darkness and terror.

'Stunning . . . an adventure story of classic quality' – *Sunday Times*

'An epic of paranoid obsession that swirls the reader headlong to deposit him on a black mudbank of horror' – *Guardian*

'As oppressive and powerful as its central character. It bursts with inventiveness' – *The Times*

World's End

London, the wilds of Corsica, a tropical island, provincial Holland . . . All are ends of the world in one way or another for the characters in this superb collection of short stories. Stranded in alien landscapes, searching for the vitality and happiness they consider their due, they are comically tragic refugees from life.

'Cruelly amusing . . . tinged with sadness . . . and composed with a stylish, sometimes savage confidence' – *Sunday Times*

'Read a story a night and you've got a fortnight's gritty dreams – and one or two nightmares' – *Time Out*

The Family Arsenal

A novel of violence in the tradition of *Brighton Rock*, set in the grimy decay of South-East London.

'One of the most brilliantly evocative novels of London that has appeared for years . . . very disturbing indeed' – Michael Ratcliffe in *The Times*

'Mr Theroux has the ability to turn the familiar into the fabulous' – Francis King in the *Sunday Telegraph*

Picture Palace

For over fifty years Maude has levelled the peepstones of her Third Eye at the beautiful, obscure and obscene, and at the private places and public parts of the famous, from Gertrude Stein to Graham Greene. At her retrospective exhibition her life, measured by camera spools, is rolled out for inspection. Except for the frame that really mattered: the exposure that should have been there, but wasn't.

'Maude's voice, harsh, coarse, and yet surprisingly innocent, remains in the ear long after the book has been put down' – *The Times*

'Too good to miss' – Auberon Waugh in the *Evening Standard*

The Old Patagonian Express

From blizzard-stricken Boston to arid Patagonia; travelling by luxury express and squalid local trucks; sweating and shivering by turns as the temperature and altitude shot up and down; thrown in with the appalling Mr Thornberry in Limon and reading nightly to the blind writer, Borges, in Buenos Aires; Paul Theroux's vivid pen clearly evokes the contrasts of a journey 'to the end of the line'.

'One of the most entrancing travel books written in our time' – C. P. Snow in the *Financial Times*

Doctor Slaughter

'Women hate me,' thought Lauren Slaughter, newly arrived in London to write a thesis on oil revenue.

But men were a different matter. Men admired – and wanted – her for her striking good looks and ability to please. She despised most of them, but she needed their money; and London had to offer more to a pretty American than a cold, uncomfortable Brixton flat.

So Lauren welcomed the anonymous introduction to Mayfair's Jasmine Escort Agency, oblivious to danger and quite unaware – until it was too late – that money was not all that was involved.

'Witty, chilly, exuberant, graphic' – *The Times Literary Supplement*

'Fairly glitters with menace' – *The Times*

The Consul's File

Paul Theroux's diplomat in *The London Embassy* began his career as resident American Consul in Malaysia ... Here is a sequence of twenty episodes in the life of Ayer Hitam in Malaysia – sharp *aperçus* of celebrated scandals, eccentricities and passions in the tiny community. The whole spectrum of life in Malaysia is evoked, from adultery to murder, from ghost stories to the vagaries of diplomatic politics, until the small town atmosphere takes on the significance of an entire world.

The London Embassy

Hero of *The Consul's File*, Theroux's American diplomat has now been promoted and posted to London. In these episodes from his career – dinner with Mrs Thatcher, meeting a Russian defector, gossip, love affairs – he infiltrates the public lives and private events of the capital's rich and famous and, in doing so, draws us a new map of London.

'Fiendishly entertaining' – *Guardian*

O-Zone

It's New Year in paranoid, computer-rich New York, and a group of Owners has jet-rotored out to party in O-Zone.

New York is a sealed city. Visits to the eerie, radioactive wasteland of O-Zone are now rarer than moon landings. The people dumped there, 'aliens', officially do not exist. For Hooper Allbright and Fizzy, Theroux's futuristic Robinson Crusoe's, the trip sets in motion an adventure of undreamed of desire and terror ...

'Extremely exciting ... as ferocious and as well-written as *The Mosquito Coast*, and that's saying something – *The Times*

'Gripping' – *Vogue*